Accounting
For
Pirates

Accounting for Pirates

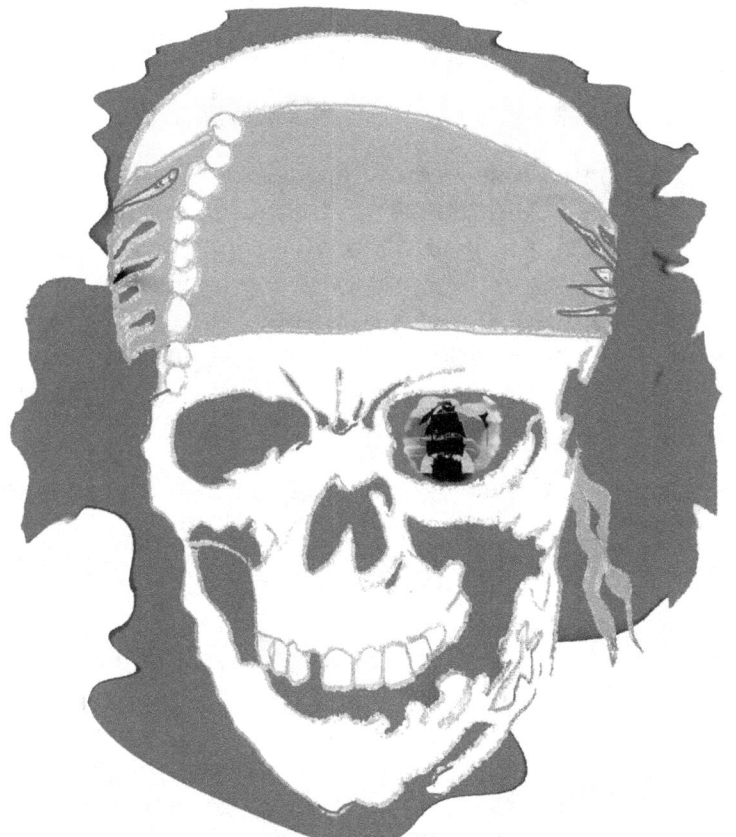

By Steve McMillan

ABSOLUTELY AMAZING eBOOKS

ABSOLUTELY AMA*ING eBOOKS

Manhanset House
Dering Harbor, New York 11965-0342

bricktower@aol.com ■ tech@absolutelyamazingebooks.com
■ absolutelyamazingebooks.com

Library of Congress Cataloging-in-Publication Data
McMillan, Steve
Accounting for Pirates
p. cm.

1. FICTION / Mystery & Detective / Amateur Sleuth
2. FICTION / Mystery & Detective / General
3. FICTION / Thrillers / Suspense

ISBN: 978-1-955036-36-8, Trade Paper
Copyright © 2022, Steve McMillan
Electronic compilation/ paperback edition
copyright © 2022 By Absolutely Amazing eBooks

Acknowledgments

Thanks to Fran, Norah, and Regina
Thanks to Shirrel, John, Terry, and Jane
Thanks to Emily, Mikayla, Mike, Matt, and Liam

And, as always, thanks to Debbi for being Debbi

Accounting
For
Pirates

Chapter One

It was a beautiful fall morning in November 1718, and Blackbeard was standing above deck on his schooner, the *Adventure*. As he watched the ocean come up on the banks of Ocracoke Island in North Carolina, he thought of all his conquests and successes as a pirate.

He recalled his birth in the southwest English town of Bristol. From there, he had been granted the right to be a privateer during Queen Anne's War against Spain from 1702 to 1713. By 1716, he had met another marauding pirate, Captain Benjamin Hornigold, in the Bahamas, and they had set up the Bahamas as "pirate central." He smiled to himself as he remembered all of their success in that area.

He had used his previous vessel, the *Queen Anne's Revenge*, to plunder his way through much of the Caribbean in early 1718. He had captured many Spanish ships during that time and taken all the booty they had had aboard. Sometimes, he found commodities such as sugar, flour, and even rum. But on several occasions, he had found what he really wanted: gold, silver, and jewels. He knew that the commodities would bring a reasonable price in the New Americas, but the valuables would make him rich beyond his fondest desires. However, he and Hornigold had decided to expand their search for treasure and come up to the Americas.

Once there, they enjoyed tremendous achievements along the coasts of Delaware and Virginia. All of his triumphs led Blackbeard to be renamed the Black-faced Devil and the Fury from Hell. As he recalled the fear he wrought, he again smiled to himself. While Blackbeard killed very few people compared to many other famous pirates, he relished in the dread that his name caused many.

In May 1718, Blackbeard had determined that he needed medical supplies as he and many of his men suffered from various diseases and maladies. So, he decided to attack

1

Charleston, South Carolina. He smiled to himself as he recalled that it had been named Blackbeard's Blockade of Charleston because he kept the city under siege for over a week until he got the medical supplies.

After Charleston, he moved up to the North Carolina coast and set up his pirate lair on Ocracoke Island. Many of his fellow pirates, such as Calico Jack Rackham and Charles Vane, joined him at Ocracoke. In fact, Ocracoke had become party central for the pirates of the Eastern Seaboard. Blackbeard recalled all the alcohol, prostitutes, and general revelry that went on for over a week. It even got its own name: The Ocracoke Orgy. He thought to himself how proud he was of that one week in particular!

As he continued to reminisce about his career as a pirate, his thoughts turned a bit dark. He knew that the governor of Virginia, Alexander Spotswood, had put a bounty on his head. It was a substantial amount, so Blackbeard knew many pirates and privateers would attempt to capture him. The one person who worried him the most was Lt. Robert Maynard, who had acquired support from the Royal Navy and His Majesty King George of England.

Blackbeard wasn't worried about getting captured by anyone other than Maynard because he knew his crew was strong and clever. Anyone who tried to board his ship would be easily repelled, or at least he thought so. But even with his natural cockiness and confidence, he had decided that he shouldn't risk his fortune in gold, silver, and jewelry.

He had three large chests full of valuable items. The chests were heavy, but he was strong. While he generally trusted his crew, they were pirates, as he was, so trust could only take you so far. Therefore, the night before, when everyone aboard was asleep, he had taken one of his small boats, loaded it with the three chests, and paddled away from where the *Adventure* was anchored. Blackbeard had an excellent memory, and he took note of the surroundings where he stopped the small boat. He took the three chests, locked them securely, and tossed them over the side. He knew the water was only about fifty feet deep in that area, so he could recover it very quickly when the time came.

As his mood changed back, thanks to feeling that his treasure was safe, Blackbeard beamed to himself. Life was good being a pirate, and he was the best. Little did he realize that he would be dead and decapitated by day's end, and his treasure lost for centuries.

Well, it would be lost until now.

Chapter Two

The Outer Banks of North Carolina are known as the Graveyard of the Atlantic. There are an estimated 2,000 shipwrecks along the border from Corolla to Ocracoke Island. This has made it a salvager's and explorer's paradise for a long time. However, in 1996, perhaps the most significant finding was uncovered: *The Queen Anne's Revenge*, the main ship of Blackbeard.

Artifacts from *The Queen Anne's Revenge* were discovered in an area close to Beaufort, N.C. Most of the findings were cannon barrels, of which it had been estimated that Blackbeard had over 40 on his ship. Other discoveries included shackles for slaves, tiny fragments of African gold, and small samples of gold dust. While the discovery had significant historical value, the much-desired lost treasure was never exposed. But all that meant was that treasure hunters continued to prowl the North Carolina shores.

The State of North Carolina restricts the number of treasure-seekers who can search in the Outer Banks area. Three hundred and twenty dives are allowed each year, and professional divers strictly supervise them. But that doesn't mean that some would-be treasure seekers don't sneak in. After all, it's a big area to cover. Noah Spencer, Jim Norman, and Henry Riddick, three recent grads from East Carolina University, were just such treasure hunters.

Noah, Jim, and Henry were all experienced divers. While most of their time was spent at their respective jobs, they always tried to work in a diving adventure now and then, looking for treasure. They had found a few items over the last couple of years that they sold for a bit of money, but nothing dramatic. But that didn't stop them from continuing to try.

Today, they were out at an area right off the coast of Ocracoke Island. They had been in this area before, but they continued to return because legend had it that this was where

Blackbeard's treasure was located. Of course, that legend was now over 300 years old, but they weren't going to be deterred. Hope springs eternal with youth!

It was a very calm Saturday in October even though it was the height of hurricane season in the Outer Banks. Noah, Jim, and Henry had taken their boat out early. They always did their diving with two in the water and one up top in case of an emergency. Today, it was Henry's turn to stay topside.

Noah and Jim had donned their wet suits and diving gear. The water wasn't that cold even though it was October, but when diving to the depths they usually did, the water got chilly pretty quickly. Noah and Jim usually tried to stay close together, but sometimes they ventured off independently. Today was one of those days.

Noah went down to the bottom and started moving the sand and silt around with his hand looking for anything of interest. Jim had found a rock formation a little way away that he wanted to explore.

Noah wasn't coming up with much. He found a few pieces of metal that looked like something someone had lost while fishing. He continued to examine the bottom, but he was getting a little low on air, so he knew he had to head to the surface soon.

Meanwhile, Jim had taken a chisel with him as he had seen this rock formation before. He was digging at the rocks to see if anything was lodged in them. All he saw were the pieces of rock that he had chipped away. Nothing important seemed to be there. But then, just as he was ready to call it, a large piece of rock broke away.

Jim looked through the murky water and reached down with his hand. He felt something metallic. He took the chisel and carefully pried away more of the rock. As the rock broke off, he saw a piece of metal under it. He wasn't sure what it was, but he continued to pry away rock until he saw that it was a container of some sort. He got really excited and swam over to Noah to get his help.

Noah and Jim loosened more of the rock, and suddenly the container became apparent, and it appeared to be a chest. They could hardly control their excitement. As they were both low on air, Jim jammed the chisel into a piece of rock to remember the location. Then they both swam to the surface.

They found they were about a hundred yards from Henry when they got to the surface. They removed their masks and yelled for him to come closer. While they waited for him, Noah said, "Did you see it? Is it what I think it is?"

Jim replied, "Don't get ahead of yourself. It could be an old trunk that has nothing of value in it. The trunk, if it's old, might be worth something, but let's not do the happy dance quite yet."

"I'm swimming in 50 feet of water. It would be hard to do the happy dance even if I wanted to," Noah said.

Once Henry arrived, they told him what they had found. They had backup air tanks on their boat, so Noah and Jim got them on and went back down. They had gotten more tools from the topside, including a hammer, screwdriver, and another chisel.

They carefully started pulling away the rock and other formations on the chest when they got below. It took some time, but after about 30 minutes, they had the chest fully exposed. They tried to lift it with their hands, but it was too heavy to reach the surface even with two of them. They went back up and got some rope they had on deck. They worked together and got the chest to raise just enough to slip the rope around it. They tied the rope off and took the other end back up to the boat. They knew they couldn't lift the chest, so they decided to drag it to the shore. They were only about 400 yards from the nearest land, so Henry used the boat to move the chest in the direction of land slowly. Noah and Jim stayed below to ensure the rope didn't slip or that the chest didn't break away.

They didn't want their boat to get stuck, so Henry stopped it when they got close to the land, and Noah and Jim pulled the chest onto the beach. It was hard work, but they could get a grip on the floor below them, so they slowly got it into the beach.

Henry anchored the boat and swam to the beach. The three of them stood around the chest and looked at each other. Noah was the first to say something, "What do you think it is?"

Noah responded, "It could just be a chest of cannonballs."

Jim smiled, "Or it could be Blackbeard's treasure."

The three smiled at each other. Henry said, "Well, it's pretty rusted, so there's no way we're going to get it open here. We need to haul it back to our truck, get it up on the truck bed, and get it home. Then we'll have more tools and can take our time getting in."

Noah said, "Blackbeard's treasure?"

Jim replied, "Yeah, probably not, but it still might have something of value in it. All I know is that we've been doing this for a while, and this is the first time we've found something that might be valuable. I'm stoked."

Little did they realize how stoked they would be once they got it open.

Chapter Three

As an accounting professor, I don't often have many exciting things happen to me. It's true that Sharon, my girlfriend who is also a Philly homicide cop, and I have had some exciting times in Malta, Belgium, Finland, and New Orleans, but those are more the exception than the rule. I primarily teach my classes, do a little research now and then, and try not to get sucked into too much academic drama at Temple University. But a very cool thing just happened.

Sharon and I were recently involved with the Dixie Mafia and money laundering in New Orleans. But it wasn't just the mafia involved, and we also had vampires or at least people who fancied them as such. Coupled with the mafia, that story got picked up in some New Orleans press and eventually got carried in some national news outlets. We didn't think that much of it, although we did do a couple of interviews for local stations in Philly. It was fun, but then we figured it would just die down, and we'd return to our everyday lives. But not so.

Recently we received an invitation to be the keynote speakers at a colloquium focusing on money laundering and how to spot it. The seminar is sponsored by several different government agencies, including the Securities and Exchange Commission, the FBI, and even the CIA. I was intrigued because it will not be a typical academic conference where you usually get strangled by endless PowerPoint presentations. And more importantly, the event is being held at the Outer Banks of North Carolina!

Neither Sharon nor I have ever been to the Outer Banks, but we have both wanted to go there for some time. It's not that far from Philly, but we have just never committed to going. I was surprised that the meeting was being held in the Outer Banks, but apparently, some of the head honchos at the SEC and FBI are natural lovers of the Outer Banks. Plus, I guess they felt that rather than a meeting, as they usually do, at some hotel or government office in D.C., they needed some distance to get some new perspectives. Essentially, I think they had just seen enough of D.C., so it was time for a change, and Sharon and I were just the beneficiaries of that need.

We were on our way down to the Outer Banks, and I was driving, and Sharon was reading up on things to do while there. I turned and said, "So, are you finding some stuff you think would be fun to do?"

"You bet! This place is different from the Jersey shore, except maybe Cape May. It's unique with a lot of things to do that wouldn't be available in Jersey."

"Like what?"

Sharon replied, "Well, there are several lighthouses, including the Cape Hatteras one, that we can climb. The Cape May Lighthouse is pretty decent, but these are bigger. Plus, they all have a lot of history. There is a massive dune called Jockey's Ridge, where Orville and Wilbur Wright did their first plane flights. We can climb the dunes or even take some hang-gliding lessons and give that a try. We could kayak on the sound or the ocean, although kayaking looks like a lot of work. And there are lots of places to try surfing or even windsurfing although the water might be a bit cool. And there are all sorts of things to see having to do with the Graveyard of the Atlantic, including taking a ferry over to Ocracoke Island to see where Blackbeard hung out."

"Blackbeard? You sure it's where Blackbeard set up shop?"

"There seems to be a lot of evidence to that effect. It looks like the locals do a lot of pirate-related re-enactments during the summer. It could just be to garner tourist money, but in 1998, divers found what they believe to be Blackbeard's ship, *The Queen Anne's Revenge*."

"Anybody find any treasure yet?" I asked.

"Apparently not much, but they did find a lot of artifacts that are valuable to museums and the like. And they're still looking. There are still enough treasure hunters around that the state of North Carolina has to limit the number of searches each year."

"All of that sounds very cool."

Sharon responded, "It does, but I have to ask you one question that I've been meaning to ask? Why do you think these mucky-mucks in all these government agencies asked us to come down? No offense, but you're an accounting professor, and I'm just a homicide cop. Surely, they have more qualified people, including themselves, who know more about money laundering than we do."

"I think it's about vampires."

"Vampires?" Sharon replied. "What do vampires have to do with it?"

"The vampire angle down in New Orleans got us noticed in the press a little bit. I doubt that the agencies expect us to tell them something they don't already know, but maybe it's so that they can say in the press or even internally that they are looking at every angle to curtail money laundering. It's a big problem, particularly with drug cartels and possible terrorist activities, and it seems the agencies haven't had much luck lately."

"So, we're window dressing?"

"Maybe, but at least we're getting a trip to the Outer Banks out of the deal. I can be 'used' as window dressing for that kind of deal."

Sharon smiled, "Good point! They can window dress me all they want, although we're driving, so no mile-high club."

I said, "Maybe we can go out on one of the beaches at night and inaugurate the dune-high club."

"I do love the way you think!"

Chapter Four

It took some effort to get the chest back to Henry's garage, but Noah, Jim, and Henry finally got it done. All three of them had to go to work that day, so the big reveal was going to have to wait a while. But they were incredibly excited, so they set up a plan to try to open the chest that night around 9 p.m.

They got to Henry's about 8:30, but they decided to wait until the appointed time. Plus, they needed to gather and sort some of the tools they had brought to get the chest open. Henry still had the chisel. Jim had brought a rubber hammer and a crowbar since they didn't want to destroy any of the chest. They knew they wanted to be careful and not just rip the thing open. Noah added an electric hacksaw in case they couldn't get the lock open and might have to cut it off.

The three assembled in Henry's garage. Noah was the first to speak. "Well, gentlemen, here is the big moment. We're going to find out if we're going to be rich or just more disappointed treasure hunters who find things for a museum, but not anything that brings wealth."

Jim added, "And I just wanted to say that I'm very proud of how hard we've worked to find this, even if it turns out not to be the mother lode. We should be pretty pleased with our efforts."

Henry said, "Absolutely! We've worked our asses off for almost two years, trying to find something of importance. Here's hoping that this is the find."

Noah also said, "Just so you guys know, I bought us a bottle of Dom Perignon champagne that is in the fridge chilling as we speak. If we do hit it big, we definitely need to celebrate."

Jim and Henry gave Noah a big high-five, and they set to work. The first thing Jim tried to do was use the crowbar to pry open the lock on the chest. He got some leverage on it, but the lock was too rusted, and he couldn't pry it open. Then Jim moved to the rubber hammer and the crowbar to pop the lock, but that didn't work either. Finally, Noah plugged the electric hacksaw in and started to work on the safety. At first, the hacksaw bounced off the rusted lock, and Noah made very little progress. But then Noah had an idea. He took the rubber hammer and chisel and banged hard on the lock to get a slight indentation in it. It wasn't a big victory, but Noah at least had a spot on the lock where he could focus the hacksaw blade.

Henry said, "Hell, this isn't working. Maybe we should try to pry open the entire lock mechanism, including what is attached to the chest."

Noah replied, "Give me just a minute. I think I'm making some progress, and we really want to minimize any damage to this thing. Even if it doesn't have riches inside, the more we keep it intact, the more valuable it is likely to be."

Henry nodded, and Noah returned to his task. The hacksaw created a lot of sparks and was slow going, but every time Noah took a break, he could see he was making some progress. After almost 30 minutes of hacksawing, Noah could see the end in sight. A few more minutes, and he felt like the lock would snap open. With that, he used the hacksaw to do the final cut in the lock, and it popped open.

Noah turned to his partners and said, "Well guys, here's the big moment." He took hold of the top of the chest and gave it a pull. Nothing! He tried again, and once again, the chest resisted.

Jim said, "Looks like the chest itself is also rusted shut. What do you guys want to do?

Henry replied, "We may have to sacrifice the chest itself some to get into what it's holding. Hand me the crowbar again, and I'll give it a whirl."

Henry pushed the crowbar up under the lid of the chest. He used the side of the rubber hammer to get some leverage. At first, it didn't seem like he was making any progress, but he said to his partners, "I can feel a little movement." He kept trying to get the lid to move, and finally, he felt one side of the chest loosen up. He moved to the other side and replicated the same process. After about 15 minutes, he felt that side of the chest also snap open. He looked up at his friends, smiled, and said, "Okay, boys. Time to see how we did." With that, Henry jerked open the chest.

The three leaned down to get a better look. They were all staring down at the contents until Noah said the first words. "Damn fellas, time to break out the Dom Perignon!"

Chapter Five

As Sharon and I made our way down to the Outer Banks, we saw billboards advertising many things to do once we got there. We knew we would be busy with the colloquium, but we hoped to get in some sightseeing.

Sharon said, "Wow, lots of things are happening down here. I guess it doesn't close down after Labor Day quite as much as the Jersey shore."

"I know there's still a lot of fishing going on, but the overall weather stays a little warmer than up our way. Can you look up the directions to where we are staying?"

Sharon pulled up the information we got about the conference. "It says we're going to be at the First Colony Inn. Says it's right on the beach road, they call it South Croatan Highway, and it's in Nags Head."

"I already looked at it some, but what do you think?"

She replied, "It looks fantastic! Definitely not your typical beachside hotel. The place was built in 1932. Has its own gardens behind the structure. It looks like it does a lot of weddings, which makes a lot of sense given how quaint, actually somewhat charming, it looks. Clearly, it's a throwback to when fewer people probably came down here, but it looks to be well maintained. Says it has a setup for meetings and retreats, so I guess that's going to be us."

"Sounds great. Are you hungry? Do you want to get something to eat before we check-in?"

"Actually, I am a little hungry. What do you want to eat? Seafood?"

I said, "If you're giving me a choice, I've always wanted to try North Carolina barbeque and hushpuppies. Supposedly they are very different from the barbeque we normally can get in the Philly area. It's dry barbeque without a ton of sauces unless you want them."

"Let me Google it and see what's around." Sharon did a quick look and said, "There is a place called Pigman's Bar-B-Que just as we're getting into the heart of the Outer Banks. It looks like it's got all the things you want."

"Point me in the right direction."

Pigman's turned out not to be on the beach road but on the causeway, yet still very convenient. We stopped and loaded up on North Carolina barbeque and hushpuppies. I even got sweet tea which is almost non-existent up where we live.

As we got back into our car, Sharon said, "Whoa, that was a lot of food. Very tasty, but pretty heavy. Maybe nap time when we get checked in."

"Works for me."

We turned off the causeway and headed towards the First Colony Inn. When we arrived, we found that the place was not very crowded, and it was easy to find a place to park. We were used to traveling pretty light, so we only had a small suitcase.

We walked in, and I said, "Wow, this is a nice place. Very impressive, but also old school. Almost looks like a huge bed and breakfast."

"It's very cool, and I'm sure we'll have a good time."

We went to the registration desk, checked in, got our key, and headed up to our room. They had us on the third floor. I opened the door to our room, and it looked even more like a B&B. Big fluffy chairs, old-style lamps, pictures of the Outer Banks, and a lovely king-sized bed.

Sharon smiled and said, "I'm all for the dune-high plan, but we may have to spend some quality time in here when we can."

"No joke. This is nice. Let's unpack, grab a quick nap, and maybe walk over to see the ocean. We've got a little time, but there is a meet and greet downstairs at 8 p.m."

We quickly unpacked our suitcases and dove into the bed. It took both of us about five minutes to conk out. We slept for about an hour and woke up at the same time. We made some coffee in the room, looked out the window at the grounds behind the hotel, and then headed out to the beach.

Crossing the beach wasn't that hard. Guess it wasn't really in season right now. We headed over to the dunes, crossed over them, and came to the ocean. I had read that the waves on the Outer Banks are more giant than much of the East Coast, and today certainly looked that way. There were a lot of surfers, boogie boarders, and even parasailers out on the water.

I asked, "So do you think we can go in?"

"As you know, I'm not much of a surfer or parasailer, but I can try some boogie boarding if we have time. Got some good waves out there."

"Yes, there are. I know we're going to be at the conference a lot of the time, but they built in some recreational time according to the schedule. We'll figure it out, but I think we'll have some fun."

We headed back to the hotel, changed into business casual attire, which the conference agenda said that was the norm, and decided to watch some TV before going down to the reception. We left our room at 8 p.m. and headed to the conference center.

We saw about 20 people, all with name tags, when we got there. We got our tags and went over to the open bar. We both got red wine and started to make the rounds. A somewhat serious-looking man who looked to be in his fifties came over to us.

"Dr. Stone and Ms. Levin. It's great that you could make it. My name is Frank Bannon, and I'm an investigator with the Securities and Exchange Commission. Welcome to the Outer Banks."

Sharon and I shook his hand, and I said, "Thanks so much for inviting us. It's an honor to be included at such a prestigious event. And both of us have also always wanted to visit the Outer Banks, so that's a big treat also. However, I'll go ahead and ask: the SEC, FBI, and CIA have so many people working on rooting out money laundering, I'm a little nervous about what we can add to the discussion."

Bannon responded, "I'm sure your adventures in New Orleans will be informative and even entertaining with the vampire angle. But to be honest, we do have something else in mind for you."

I quizzically asked, "Uh oh, and what would that be?"

"We want you to be a part of determining if audit firms are actually doing their jobs. We want you to join the Public Company Accounting Oversight Board, the PCAOB."

I stood with a shocked look on my face and said to Sharon. "Well, I didn't see that one coming."

Chapter Six

Noah opened the bottle of champagne as the three treasure hunters surveyed their find. They all grabbed a plastic cup, poured some bubbly, and toasted their good fortune. Jim said, "Hot damn, fellas. We have hit the mother lode. Look at all this gold, silver, and jewels."

Henry said, "I don't even know where to start. It's amazing."

Noah said, "Before we start plowing through all of this, I think we need to figure out our overall plan. Like how are we going to make sure all of this stays with us? There's a fortune here, and if anyone finds out about it, there are plenty of thieves and the like who will look to come take it from us."

Jim replied, "You're right! I was so excited about the find that protecting it never crossed my mind. Plus, how are we going to make money out of it? We can't just sell it piece by piece to pawn shops. There aren't that many pawn shops in this area."

Noah said, "Well, the first thing I think we need to decide is if we're telling anyone else about it? My vote is no, including our families. The more people who know about it, the more likely someone will try to steal it from us. Or even the State of North Carolina will say it has ownership because we found it in an area that the state likely owns."

"Maybe we should tell the state," asked Henry. "Could be a reward or something for it."

Noah replied, "If there is some sort of reward, it's not going to be anything like selling it as far as money goes. And if the state finds out, they'll probably at least try to tie us up with paperwork and even lawsuits before we can actually get the money. I think we keep it to ourselves and start doing a little research on what some of the pieces might be worth. Does anyone feel guilty about not donating it all to the state for historic preservation?" Henry and Jim shook their heads in unison.

Jim said, "Do you think we just hide it here? What happens if someone in my family happens upon it?"

"Good question," replied Noah. "We need someplace safe where we can hide it for the time being until we figure out what to do next."

Jim said, "Both of you know that I had a hidey-hole behind the garage at my family's house. When I was little, I dug the hole with my dad to hide there and play games with people. It's still there, but none of us ever use it anymore. In fact, I doubt anyone in my family really even remembers it. It is just a hole with a few pieces of wood on the walls with a metal cover. I haven't been down there in years, but it might still be usable. We could go over tonight and check it out."

Henry inquired, "What happens if someone in your family sees us do it?"

Jim said, "Well if we get some containers to split the loot in, it's pretty heavy as it is with everything in the chest. I'll go over to see my parents and keep them occupied while you two get the containers into the hole. It may not be a long-term solution, but we can't just leave it in this garage. It may take us a while to figure out how to get the most money for us out of this find."

Noah suggested, "I like the idea of splitting it up, but maybe we should also take a few small containers to each one of our apartments. We really don't want to keep all of this in one place. If somehow someone does find the big haul, we would still have some of the treasure left."

"That's a good idea," said Henry. "We all have places we could hide some smaller containers somewhere in our apartments. Maybe we keep the bulk in the hidey-hole but have some spread out to lower our risk of losing it all." They all agreed with that idea.

Jim smiled, "Well, gentlemen, I think we have a plan. How about we finish off our champagne and start going through the chest. Let's see what kind of goodies we've uncovered. I don't know about you two, but I doubt I'm going to sleep any tonight. We're rich, and I like it. I don't think this will be the last time we indulge in Dom Perignon."

With that, the three clinked their plastic cups together and downed the last of the champagne. It was time to figure out how rich they had suddenly become!

Chapter Seven

Sharon looked at me and said, "Okay, what the hell is the PCAOB?"

Bannon smiled and said, "Well, Ben, do you want to do the honors, or shall I?"

I said, "I'll give it a try, but if I miss something, please feel free to chime in."

Bannon nodded.

"PCAOB stands for Public Company Accounting Oversight Board. Back in the early 2000s, there were several very prominent accounting and financial scandals. Probably the biggest was Enron down in Houston. Enron started as an oil and natural gas supplier. No big deal as there were a lot of these types of companies in the 1990s. But Enron moved away from existing pipelines, trucks, and the like and started developing financial instruments based on oil, natural gas, and eventually electricity. It was a tremendous innovation, and Enron became very wealthy, particularly senior management, as did its employees. But it all turned out to be a lie!"

"Enron's CEO, Jeff Skilling, started to use a particular accounting method called mark-to-market. Without getting too technical, Enron could book profits that were never going to be actually realized. And they did a lot of this. Right before their collapse, they were worth $65 billion on paper."

Sharon queried, "But I know enough about what you do to ask: I thought auditors were there to make sure the financial statements are correct?"

Bannon and I looked at each other and couldn't help but smile. I said, "That's exactly what they are supposed to do. And the big firms get paid a lot of money to do it. But some of them decided to cheat, particularly one of the largest firms, Arthur Andersen. Andersen was the auditor for Enron, and they signed off on all sorts of illegal accounting activities.

In fact, in 2001, when Enron started to blow up, Andersen shredded tons of incriminating documents. But both they and Enron got caught, many Enron execs went to jail and paid huge fines, and when it was all over, Andersen didn't exist any longer."

"They went out of business?"

"They were forced out of business, and many of their partners had to pay huge fines even though they had nothing to do with Enron. Back then, if you were a partner in an accounting firm, you were a general partner, which meant that all your assets were at risk if something bad happened. And something terrible happened with Enron and Arthur Andersen."

Sharon asked, "So people who had nothing to do with Enron lost their jobs?"

Bannon stepped in, "Yes, 28,000 of them, more or less."

"28,000 people lost their jobs over something they had nothing to do with?"

I said, "He's right, and there were other scandal-ridden firms during that period. WorldCom took down over 20,000 people. And just as an aside, Andersen was their auditor, too. But all of this affected more than just a few companies and one auditor. Suddenly, no one on Wall Street believed the financial statements coming out, and if you don't believe the financial statements, you don't invest. The stock market dived."

"Okay, and forgive my language, but this sounds like some pretty serious shit!" said Sharon.

Bannon smiled and said, "It was some dire shit, and that's why the government needed to step in."

"What did they do?' asked Sharon.

Bannon said, "Go ahead, you take it, Ben."

"In 2002, Congress passed the Sarbanes-Oxley Act. The act tightened up the laws for public companies, including adding criminal penalties for corporate officers who falsify financial statements. Before Sarbanes-Oxley about all you could do was fine the corporate officers. However, most of these folks made so much money, and you couldn't fine them enough to hurt them. But now, they could go to jail. In addition, Sarbanes-Oxley established the PCAOB to ensure the auditors follow the correct audit procedures and guidelines. The PCAOB is under the direction of the SEC."

Sharon said, "So the PCAOB basically audits the auditors."

I replied, "In a way. The PCAOB makes sure that auditors are following the correct audit procedures. But it's a tough job because we are down to only four big accounting firms, and those firms have a lot of clients. And because many of the companies are so huge, there are still many areas in which an auditor has an immense amount of discretion on how to characterize a certain part of an audit. The firms being audited are so big that the auditors can't go through each transaction, so they must rely on internal controls. And that's where the auditors have some leeway that can dramatically affect the financial results. The PCAOB is supposed to make sure that the audit firms aren't bending or even breaking the rules."

Sharon looked a bit shocked. "So, you mean to say that after Enron and Andersen and all the other scandals, you still can't always trust the financial statements?"

I said, "Trust to an extent. It is unlikely that an accounting firm would do something as egregious as Andersen did. Still, there is a lot of pressure on auditors to deliver the financial statements that the company wants. And even though there are only four big firms left, a company can still change auditors if they want. Auditors can't just give it away as Andersen did, but there are still a lot of gray areas. The PCAOB is supposed to minimize those gray areas. And to you, Frank, I thought it was doing a decent job."

"Ben, I wish that were true, but it's not. In fact, we just found out that KPMG hired a PCAOB official who fed KPMG information on how to look the best for a PCAOB inspection. Two or three KPMG employees and the PCAOB person involved will be indicted and perhaps sent to jail. But why I'm here and talking to you is that this KPMG scandal gives the PCAOB a black eye. Not much a watchdog if you're not watching or giving out the code to get past the security. So, we are looking at a pretty big overhaul of the agency, and we're seeking input from knowledgeable practitioners and academics on how best to restructure the agency."

I said, "Okay, Frank, that makes sense, but come on, I'm a prof at Temple University. I love Temple, but it ain't Stanford or Harvard. Surely you can get much bigger names than mine to help you out with this."

"You're being a bit modest because you have done some decent accounting work, but you're right. We could get some big names. But that's not what we want. Most of the big-name accounting practitioners and academics do a ton of consulting on the side and probably even do side work for some of the audit firms we examine. Once I saw the story about New Orleans, I did a little digging on you. You do a few tax returns now and then, and you do some work with Sharon and the Philly police, but you seem satisfied with doing that and not expanding to bigger fish. In short, I don't see you having a bunch of conflicts of interest, and that makes you very attractive to SEC."

"So, bringing us down to talk about New Orleans and money laundering was a bit of a false flag. You wanted to pitch me on the PCAOB."

"Not a total false flag. We really are interested in what happened in New Orleans, but, yes, we did have another motive. Not completely a scam because we could have just come to your office at Temple to pitch you on the PCAOB job. Two birds, as they say, with the trip down here. Anyway, what's your initial reaction?"

"Not sure. Why don't we go get some drinks, and we can talk about it some more, and maybe I can mull it over a bit."

"Drinks always work for me when Ben starts talking accounting," said Sharon. "Race you guys to the bar."

Chapter Eight

While we were sitting at the bar, Frank introduced some of the other participants to us

"Dr. Ben Stone and Detective Sharon Levin, I would like you to meet George Thomas and Linda Rankin, who work with me at the SEC." We all shook hands. "Next, we have Emily Keen and Randall Jones of the FBI." More handshakes. "And finally, Matthew Bender, Liam Franks, and Debbi Wilson of the CIA." A final round of handshakes.

Sharon asked, "CIA? I thought the CIA only dealt with foreign criminal activities and has no domestic authority?"

Debbi chimed in, "That's indeed what our mandate is, but many times these large money laundering schemes cross many countries, and the CIA has assets throughout the world that can be of assistance."

I inquired, "So, the FBI and CIA work together?"

Debbi smiled, "I know. If you watch a lot of cop and spy shows on TV, it looks like we are constantly fighting for jurisdiction and credit, but it's really not that way. There are indeed plenty of egos in both agencies, but we can most of the time collaborate fairly well towards the end of curbing money laundering. As I'm sure you know, money laundering is a huge problem internationally and domestically, and there is a lot of cross-fertilization. Plus, a lot of laundered money funds terrorist activities, and that's a big part of what the CIA focuses on these days. It's almost mandatory we work together with the FBI."

I grinned and said, "So, Frank sort of conned me a little about coming here because he has another request he wants me to consider. You folks hiding anything in your back pockets you want us to do?"

Everyone snickered. Emily said, "Can't speak for the CIA, but the FBI is here only about laundering money. That is unless Sharon wants to apply to Quantico to be an FBI agent?"

"No, thanks, I'm good where I am."

Liam spoke for the CIA. "We're being straight with you, also, although we could use some top-shelf accounting help if Ben has any interest?"

I laughed, "Never pass the polygraph. But I'm still a little shocked that all of you came here to talk about money laundering. Just like I said about the SEC, surely you have agents who know as much or more than Sharon and I can provide."

"I'll admit that a little getaway from D.C. factored into our interest," said Emily. "Things have been really crazy of late at the Bureau, and we hope having a few days away from the office can be restorative."

"Pretty much the same at the CIA," said Matthew. "All three of us have been in many, many different time zones of late, and just hanging at the beach, but not having to take vacation days to do it, looked very attractive."

Sharon chuckled, "Our tax dollars at work. Just kidding, I sometimes use Ben's job to get a little R&R for myself without dipping into my vacation time. Gotta take care of ourselves sometimes."

I said, "Well, since this event starts pretty early tomorrow, maybe we should have another drink or two and then call it a night. You folks from the CIA and FBI are probably more used to all-nighters than we are. Stakeouts and the like."

Emily smiled and said, "I got my start as a street cop in Albuquerque. When I made detective, I pulled my share of stakeouts, so I'm guessing Sharon has drawn a few overnights."

"That's true, although it's been a while since I pulled an overnight. But, yeah, I've lived off coffee for 48 hours or more before. Thankfully, most of my cases of late haven't required that level of coffee intake."

Liam said, "It's still pretty warm outside, and the sky is beautiful. Why don't we get another round and go outside and talk about anything other than work? Maybe compare the Eagles to the Washington Football Team. By the way, I wish they would just pick a name because this football team thing is looking more and more ridiculous as time goes on."

Everyone chuckled, and I said, "You're right, Liam. Let's get a round and go outside and try to hear the ocean. We'll get enough work talk in over the next few days."

With that, all of us grabbed a drink and headed to the patio. Since I was the only person not involved in some sort of law enforcement-type job, I'm sure they all figured this would be an easy gig compared to their usual jobs. And it would be for everyone but Sharon and me.

Chapter Nine

Noah, Jim, and Henry quickly got the booty all spread out. They hid the bulk of it at Jim's house in his little hidey-hole. However, they followed through with their plan of keeping some of it safeguarded at each of their apartments.

All three picked pieces from their caches to research and start looking for the types of baubles and any value estimates. Noah took a gold bracelet, Jim decided on a bar of gold, and Henry went with a large silver flask. They decided to meet at Noah's place to debrief on what they found out.

The next night, they huddled at Noah's house. Noah got it started with, "So, you guys have any luck so far?"

Jim replied, "I guess I had the easiest one to do. I weighed the gold bar, and it came in at four and a half pounds. Gold is trading at about $23,000 per pound, so I'm coming in at a little over $100,000. But that's just the gold price. Since we think this gold may go back to Blackbeard's time, the antique value may mean that it's worth a whole lot more. But it's easy to say it's worth a least $100K.

Henry said, "I started with the same idea. The silver flask weighed in at a little over 12 pounds. Silver is only going for about $300 per pound, so I've only got about $4,000 of just silver. But I did a little research on Google and found that a similar type of vessel was sold at Sotheby's for over $150,000 because of its historical value. There seems to be great demand for silver that has some historical significance. Truthfully, I think we could easily get at least $100,000 for it, but perhaps much more."

Finally, Noah weighed in with, "I guess I sort of had the hardest one to value. The gold by itself is probably not worth that much, but I found a similar bracelet at Sotheby's. That bracelet was dated at about the 1700s and believed to be from England. According to the Sotheby website, they couldn't determine the original owner, but it has an inscription indicating an English royalty provenance. Still, they're not sure which royal family member had it. Because of that, the price came in at $250,000. I did a little more research, and I think that if they could prove it once was worn by the wife of George III, King of England, then the price would be over a million and maybe even more. But if Sotheby's can't get the provenance needed, I doubt we will, so I'd say we're looking at $250K. But that's still pretty decent!"

Jim said, "So we're at almost a half a million, and we're just getting started. Boy, fellas, this may be even bigger than I thought it would be. But I still don't quite have it figured out how we will sell this stuff. I'm pretty sure we could try Sotheby's or Christie's, but then we would have to explain how we found it. I don't think we broke any laws, but I'm not a lawyer, so I'm not sure."

Henry said, "And we've already discussed that there could be a risk that the State of North Carolina comes in and claims it for historical reasons. However, I researched the Queen Anne's Revenge and found that they've been pulling up from the Nags Head area, and the divers who found those artifacts have been getting paid, but they've found no jewels, gold, and the like. They've found cannons and cannonballs, which are important but certainly less valuable than the stuff we've found."

Noah said, "Okay, I know it's a risk, but I do know a pawn shop owner up in Kill Devil Hills. His name is Fred Biltmore. My dad has done some business with him over the years, and I went to high school with his son, Bobby. I'm pretty sure Bobby works in the shop with his dad. They're pretty nice guys and have a reputation for being honest.

"How about we try this?" suggested Jim, "Noah takes the bracelet and silver flask into the pawnshop. The gold is a bit obvious, so that stays. Noah tells Bobby and his dad that he found it in his grandmother's basement or somewhere and wants to get an idea of what they might be worth. We've already done a little research and have at least some clues of worth, so we'll get an idea of how honest these guys are and whether we are way off base. I like the research we've done, but we're still doing a lot of guessing. If the pawn guys are way off what we think the value is, we'll know we need to get another appraisal, maybe from a jewelry store. But we've still got to be careful because we don't want it to get out that we have this haul, at least not yet. While Noah does that, we take a bit of a chance, and Henry and I will take the gold bar over to the North Carolina Maritime Museum. We'll tell them we found it off the coast of Ocracoke while diving. We'll find out the state rules on whether it's finder's keeper's and what happens if it's not. We'll at least get an idea of how public we can be with the find, and maybe even find out that we can cash out with the museum. Right now, we just have to get more information than we have."

"That sounds like a great plan," said Noah. "We get input from more sources, and then we can have some idea of what the next steps might be. But don't forget, guys, we need to keep this on the QT until we have an overall plan."

Henry smiled and said, "Mum's the word!"

Chapter Ten

Sharon and I were up early because we wanted to get some coffee and walk on the beach before the program began. It was chilly outside, but the water and the waves were still beautiful.

We knew from the program that business casual was the suggested attire for the conference. I had my usual khaki pants, polo shirt, and boat shoes. Sharon decided to go in a pants suit and flats. She said there was no reason to break out the FM shoes.

We saw coffee and bagels set out when we reached the conference room. We counted 20 or so attendees, including the eight we had met the day before. Everyone seemed to be just mingling for a few minutes. I saw name badges available on a table, so I retrieved ours.

From the SEC, Frank Bannon and Linda Rankin talked, smiled, and both came over to us. Frank said, "Good morning to both of you. Sleep well?"

Sharon replied, "Splendid. I think I could hear the waves even from our room. The ocean always puts me out."

"Same here," said Linda. "I have a white noise machine I use at home. I live in Fairfax, which is usually pretty quiet, but I've gotten used to the white noise machine, and I typically pick the ocean as my white noise."

"I live downtown in Philly so that it can get a little noisy at night. I usually have a fan on, even in the winter. At first, Sharon thought I was nuts, but now she seems to like it."

"I do. I live down in South Philly, not far from South Street. South Street is filled with restaurants and bars that are very loud at night. I was pretty used to it, but when Ben and I got together, I grew accustomed to the fan, and I use one now, too."

I asked, "So who is in charge of this shindig?"

Frank replied, "Actually, you met her. Emily Keen is the one who orchestrated this event, and she's the one handling all of the logistics. She'll be introducing everyone soon."

Right at that moment, Emily asked everyone to take a seat. She opened with, "Thank all of you for coming. I know that we have representatives from the SEC, FBI, and CIA in attendance. Also, our keynote speakers are Dr. Ben Stone from Temple University and Detective Sharon Levin from the Philadelphia Homicide Division, who are up tomorrow. As most of you know, Ben and Sharon were involved in a major bust down in New Orleans, including money laundering and vampires. Yes, that's what I said, vampires. Not real vampires, at least I don't think they were, but some young people who took the vampire thing very, very seriously." There was a soft chuckle in the crowd. "Anyway, what we want to accomplish here is to exchange some information about important laundering cases we've all had, get to know each other, and enjoy the Outer Banks, not necessarily in that order. We're going to knock off at about 3 p.m. so that people can enjoy the Outer Banks some. We have dinner at 8 pm at the Jolly Roger Restaurant in Kill Devil Hills. As many of you know, the FBI is picking up the tab, which happens about once every millennium. Anyway, anyone got any questions before we get started?"

I raised my hand and said, "You got the FBI to foot the bill? All I can say is thanks because, in academia, no one ever picks up the tab for a conference dinner."

"As I noted, it doesn't often happen with the FBI, but we just had a huge laundering bust happen up in Boston. We're going to talk some about it later today. The higher-ups were feeling generous since we got a lot of positive press about that bust. It always helps if you can do something that makes the bureau look good."

Emily continued and said, "Anyway, get some more coffee, hit the head if you need to, and we'll get started. The CIA is up first with a laundering scheme that includes Colombia, Mexico, and even the Jamaican mob. I hope everyone finds it interesting and informative."

Sharon and I smiled at each other. She whispered, "Probably not as exciting as Malta, Belgium, and Finland, and no mile-high club, but I'll bet it's still pretty interesting. Plus, the dune-high club could be nice."

I nodded my head. Time to go to work.

Chapter Eleven

Early the following day, Noah took the bracelet and flask over to the Biltmore Pawn Shop. He recognized the son, Bobby, as soon as he walked in the door.

He walked over and said, "Bobby Biltmore! It's Noah Spencer. It's been a long time!"

"Noah, it has been a long time." They shook hands and even did a little man hug. "What brings you into the store?"

"I have a couple of antique items that I want your dad to look at. Is he in?"

"He just made a coffee run. I should be back in a few minutes. What are you doing with yourself these days?"

Noah replied, "I'm working with a small real estate company over towards Manteo. I do some apartment selling, and sometimes I help get the apartments ready to be shown. A little manual labor, but nothing too heavy. I'm doing it to bring in a little dough as I have a small apartment over in Manteo."

"Living by yourself? No girlfriend involved?"

"Yep, living by myself right now. It's just a studio apartment. No full-time girlfriend, but I occasionally get lucky and have a sleepover. Not as much as I would like, of course, but still doing okay."

"Do you still go diving with Jim and Henry?"

"We do. We haven't been in a while since we all have full-time jobs, but we try to work it in when we can. As I'm sure you know, water is getting colder, so got to break out the wetsuits. I see you're working with your dad. Still living at home, or have you got your own place?"

Bobby said, "As you may remember, my dad has a finished basement, and I've set up shop there for the time being. I like working for him, it pays the bills, but my long-term plan is to head to the islands, maybe Jamaica, to open a small dive shop."

"Really, you've been doing a lot of diving?"

"I have. I got all the certifications to be a dive instructor. Living with my dad, I've saved a little money, so I think I can open a small shop. I've made a few trips to Jamaica over the last few years and met some people in the dive business."

"That sounds great. I wish I had a better plan. Sort of just treading water right now."

Bobby smiled, "Oh, I have a plan, and I'm excited about it, but it's a long way from being a done deal."

Just then, Bobby's dad, Fred, walked into the shop. He recognized Noah immediately. "Noah Spencer, it's been forever since I've seen you." With that, Fred put out his hand.

"Mr. Biltmore, it has been a long time," as Noah extended his hand. "The shop looks great. It looks like you and Bobby have been doing pretty well."

"Business comes and goes, but it's been okay. Many tourists come into the shop, figuring that we have all sorts of pirate antiques and collectibles since we are in the Outer Banks. We have a little, but we have more Rolexes, fake Rolexes, and costume jewelry. But I can't complain. Keeping a roof over our house. What brings you in?"

"Well, sir, I was looking through a box that my grandmother left when she passed. It was in her basement, and when her house was sold, I found it as we were cleaning out the old stuff. The box didn't look that important at the time, so it's been sitting in our basement. The other day I was looking for some of my old diving gear and happened upon the box. Obviously, I knew it wasn't my gear, but I just decided to look through it. Top half of the box had clothes in it, but as I looked further, I found a piece of antique jewelry and a flask. I was wondering if you could take a look at them and tell me if you think they're worth anything?"

"Sure," said Fred, "Happy to help. Let me see them."

Noah handed over the bracelet and the flask. Fred decided to look at the flask first. He whistled and said, "Wow, Noah, this is some expensive stuff you have here. Clearly, this is sterling silver which would be worth something on its own but look at the engravings on the bottom, particularly the date. I can't be sure it's not a fake because I'm not an expert, but this looks to be at least three hundred or so years old if it's genuine. If it's 300 years old, it's worth a ton."

Fred put the flask down and picked up the bracelet. He took his jewelry loop out and scrutinized the piece. He put the bracelet down, went to a website, and did some clicking. After a couple of minutes, he whistled again and said, "And this might be worth even more, Noah."

"Really?"

"Well, I know this is eighteen-carat gold, and these are rubies and diamonds. Again, worth a good bit just on those facts alone. But look at the engraving on the back here. It's a little hard to see, but with the loop, you can make out a name: William Blake."

Noah leaned in and said, "Yeah, I think I can see it. Why is he a big deal?"

"Big doesn't do him justice. That's why I had to Google it because I had to be sure of the name. William Blake was one of the most renowned British jewelers of the 16th and 17th centuries. I mean biggest of the big. I only know anything about him because I watch both the U.S. and British versions of *Antiques Roadshow*. I remember seeing a small brooch that had his name on it. The appraiser almost fainted when he saw the name. He appraised this little piece at over $250,000 but said that with a little more authentication, the sky's the limit for something like this. Hell, Noah, how did your grandmother afford things that cost this much? You got a big trust fund that we don't know about?"

"No trust fund. And I have no idea how she came across these things. We were very middle class growing up, so my granddad could not afford anything like this. I'm shocked that these two pieces are worth so much. Are you sure?"

"Not positive because I own a pawn shop in the Outer Banks and don't work with Sotheby's and Christie's. You would need someone with much more experience and expertise than I have to be sure, but I can tell you they are worth a bunch. I don't know how much of a bunch, but definitely a bunch? Congratulations."

"Thanks. I appreciate your help."

"Well, Noah, obviously I can't afford to offer you anything close to what these are worth, but it's been a treat to see them. Do you have anything else?"

"No, sir. These are the only pieces I've found."

Bobby, who had been following the conversation, looked closely at Noah's face as he said there wasn't anything else. Bobby didn't believe it for a second. He had a feeling there had to be more. Maybe a lot more. But, more importantly, Bobby knew some guys who might be able to help find out if there was more.

The Jamaican mob is very good at finding things.

Chapter Twelve

The first day of the conference was exciting. Sharon and I learned a lot about international money laundering, particularly from the CIA. The FBI went into depth about their big bust in Boston, and the SEC did a bit about how some of the big banks, the so-called money center banks, had been involved in some laundering schemes in the Cayman Islands. The dinner at the Jolly Roger was very informal, and somewhat surprisingly, everyone seemed to enjoy each other's company. There was no rivalry between the agencies. In short, it was fun. But that night, Sharon and I agreed that we were a little worried about whether our presentation would pass muster.

We got to the conference room a little early to set up our computers and get our game faces on. As a prof, I had done many presentations, and of course, lectured a lot, but Sharon had done very little of this. I could see she was nervous as we got ready.

"Babe, don't worry. You have to remember that you know more about this topic than anyone else in the room, other than me. They all know a lot about money laundering, but not exactly how we caught the launderers. And none of them know as much about vampires as we do!"

"Okay," said Sharon, "That's a bit of comfort, but I'm not sure I can command an audience talking about vampires."

"You'll do great. Plus, we're opening with it. We've got a story to tell and not just a mind-numbing stack of PowerPoint slides to plow through."

"Okay, but don't wander off. If I start to get stuck, feel free to jump right in."

"You won't need me, but I've got your six."

"You've got my six? I think we've been watching a few too many cop shows."

As all the other participants came in and got coffee and snacks, Sharon and I said hello to them. Everyone found their seats, and Emily introduced us. "So, as everyone here knows, our speakers this morning are Dr. Ben Stone from Temple University and Detective Sharon Levin from the Philadelphia Homicide Division. Just a bit of background, Ben is a professor of accounting and has been at Temple for 15 years. His academic interest is financial accounting, mainly accounting measures to predict economic outcomes. He has been a white-collar crime consultant for the Philly cops for several years. Sharon is from Philadelphia and has been on the police force for almost 20 years. She started as a beat cop and worked her way up to homicide detective.

"As you know, Ben and Sharon are going to tell us about their exploits in New Orleans, but they have had many adventures together, particularly internationally. In Malta, a small archipelago in the Med, they got involved with cryptocurrency, if you didn't know. In Belgium, they had some Russian mob adventures, while in Finland, they helped capture a female serial killer. I've got to say, Ben, not bad for an accounting professor. Anyway, my understanding is that Sharon is going to kick us off, so Sharon, please take the stage." There was polite applause.

Sharon stood and moved to the podium. "Well, good morning, everyone. I need to warn you upfront that I haven't done much of this, but I'll do my best. Anyway, let me start with: Does anyone here believe in vampires?"

No one immediately raised their hand. Sharon added, "Okay, does anyone here like vampire books and movies?"

A lot of hands went up. "Okay, since Emily's hand went up first, I'll ask her: Of vampire books and movies, which ones do you like the best?"

Emily replied, "I've always enjoyed the Anne Rice books and movies the most. I've watched some old vampire movies, and I think they're pretty good, too, but *Interview with the Vampire* is my favorite. I also enjoy and still watch for Halloween, *30 Days of Night,* about vampires in Alaska where it stays dark for so long. I've always thought that was a great premise. And I've been to Alaska on assignment, although not as far north as Barrow where the movie takes place."

"Funny you mention *30 Days of Night* because I've always enjoyed that, too, although I haven't been to Alaska. Anyway, for the record, Ben and I don't believe that vampires exist, but in New Orleans, we found a group that certainly felt they were," Sharon said.

"The coven, that's what they called themselves, in New Orleans was made up of two young men and one young woman. They didn't believe they could live forever, and they went out in the daylight, but they firmly believed that drinking another human's blood would give them more energy and power. New Orleans has an estimated 50 or so vampires who get small amounts of blood from willing participants. These three didn't think that was enough, so they started knocking people out with chloroform, drinking a lot of their blood and then killing them using a knife. The three were very successful with their first two killings, and the cops didn't have much to go on. However, and all of you know this that luck is sometimes the most important thing in breaking a case, their third victim was the chief accountant for the Dixie Mafia."

Frank Bannon of the SEC asked, "The Dixie Mafia? What is that?"

Sharon responded, "It's not like the Italian or Jewish mob from up north. It's a loosely organized group of mobsters down south who traffic in drugs, racketeering, and gambling. They're not part of a family like up north, and they don't take a blood oath about secrecy. But they have been around for a while, and their influence comes and goes. They make a lot of illegal money, and they need to launder it, so that's where Ben came in. But before I turn it over to Ben, what happened was that the accountant left a lot of files, the Dixie Mafia found out about the vampires, they worried that the vamps might know something, so they were going after them. Ben and I saw the third killing from afar when we were out walking, so the Dixie Mafia also came after us. We warded them off, but that got us involved with the New Orleans police, and that's when Ben got involved. Ben, you're up."

"So, my role was to examine some of the accountant's records. The NOLA police have a forensic accountant they normally use for such things, but he was traveling and unavailable. I took a look at the records and determined that the money laundering was likely taking place at a casino. I'm sure all of you know that casinos worldwide are prevalent laundering locales—lots of cash and many times shaky security policies. New Orleans has one big casino, and we figured that's where they went. We set up surveillance and caught the launderers in the act. Naturally, the launderers lawyered up, but the NOLA police, with Sharon's help, squeezed them enough that they wanted a deal, and what they could offer was that they had tracked down the wannabe vampires and were willing to give them up. The NOLA police raided the vampires' apartment and found enough evidence to arrest them. The last we heard, they were convicted of murder one, sentenced to execution, but are appealing the verdict. As you probably know, Louisiana still has the death penalty, so they are going to be locked up for a while before anything else happens."

Frank said, "So you helped capture three murderers and assisted in breaking up a money-laundering scheme. Not a bad day's work."

Sharon smiled and said, "Just another day at the office for the team of Levin and Stone."

I said, "Levin and Stone?"

"Yeah, we're going in alphabetical order." There was a chuckle around the room.

"But the NOLA police and the FBI are still combing through the accountant's records and finding more evidence of money laundering. This might turn out to be a big win for them. I think my efforts should mean that I go to the head of the class."

"Yeah, but I'm the one who saved us from being kidnapped and possibly killed by the Dixie Mafia. Because of that alone, I get to be first. Also, I'm the one who carries a gun." More laughter.

"Fine, but the next time we have a murder investigation, I call dibs on being at the top of the letterhead."

Little did we know how quickly that subsequent murder investigation would begin!

Chapter Thirteen

Bobby Biltmore was generally a good guy. He'd never been in any real trouble. Went to a few parties that got out of hand, and the cops came. Had a couple of speeding tickets. Even got pulled one time when he had been drinking, but the cop knew Bobby's dad, so he had Bobby leave his car, and the cop took him home. Didn't cite him for a DUI, so Bobby got off easy.

But Bobby had this dream of going to the islands, likely Jamaica, and starting a dive business. He had exaggerated to Noah how much he had saved for that adventure. He had a little money put away, but he needed a big chunk of dough before that dream could become a reality. However, he had an idea of how he might expedite that effort.

Bobby had made a couple of trips to Jamaica, but he had primarily stayed at the resorts. Thus, he didn't think he really had a flavor for living down there. Back up at the Outer Banks, he had met two guys from Jamaica, Winston Whyte, and Fitzroy Reed, who were working the fishing business over in Wanchese. Since Bobby had wanted to know more about Jamaica, he had bought a few rounds of drinks one time for the two. While mostly they had talked about reggae music, women, and rum, they had talked a little about how to start a business down there. Winston said a lot of the dive business down in Jamaica was controlled by Lloyd Sinclair, a local organized crime figure. Winston said that Sinclair had many illegal businesses, but mostly he was into drugs. Sinclair never really cared about making money in the dive business because he had a real fascination with buried treasure, particularly Blackbeard, who reportedly spent a lot of time in Jamaica and perhaps left some treasure behind. Sinclair had paid for a number of dive attempts looking for treasure but had come up with very little. But Winston said that if Bobby

53

wanted to have a successful dive operation, he would have to get to know Sinclair. It would be dangerous to do otherwise.

Bobby was off on a Friday, and he knew that the fishing boats would be coming in about 5 pm. He didn't know exactly which one Whyte and Reed would be on because the ship's hands rotated from boat to boat. But he knew that if he just hung around the dock when the boats came in, he was likely to see them.

Around 4:30, Bobby saw a large fishing boat head into port. From the look of the deck, the boat had made a good haul that day of tuna, so it was likely that everyone on board would be in a good mood. They would be smelly but in a good mood.

After the boat docked, Bobby got a look at the crew and saw that Whyte and Reed were indeed on this boat. He waved to them, and they waved back although they looked a little confused about who it was, and then they came ashore.

Bobby met them. "Winston, Fitzroy, how are you guys doing? You remember me, don't you? Bobby Biltmore with the pawnshop."

Winston said, "Oh yeah, you bought us a few rounds to talk about starting a dive business down in Jamaica."

"Yep, that's me. It looks like you guys had a good day fishing."

Fitzroy said, "We were due for one. Haven't had many big hauls lately, but yeah, today we did okay. What are you doing here?"

Bobby replied, "I was wondering if I could buy you guys another couple of rounds after you clean up. I've got news that I'd like to share with you and get your take on what to do next."

Winston said, "Always up for free drinks. Give us about an hour, and we'll meet you over at Sam and Omie's."

"I'll see you then."

Bobby decided to go up to Pigman's BBQ to get some food. Sam and Omie's had bar food, but he was hungry. It took him about an hour to get his food, eat it, and get back down to Sam and Omie's, which was on the island's south side.

He went into Sam and Omie's and looked around for Winston and Fitzroy, but they weren't there yet. He got a draft Bud and waited at the bar.

After about 15 minutes, Winston and Fitzroy came in together. Everyone shook hands, and Bobby bought a round of Buds, and they headed outside since the weather was still pretty nice.

After they sat, Winston asked, "So Bobby, what's up that you want to talk to us about?"

"Well, as you probably know, my dad owns a pawn shop, and we had a guy come in the other day with some jewelry and a silver flask. My dad looked at them and thought they were likely to be very valuable. He even said that the jewelry piece looked like it might be pirate treasure."

Both Winston and Fitzroy perked up. Fitzroy said, "So he had two pieces?"

"Yeah, he said he found them in his grandmother's stuff, but I don't believe it. I know his family well, and if they had really had anything that looked as valuable as these pieces did, they would have long ago sold them. Plus, this is just a guess, but I think he has more. It just seemed that way from looking at him."

Winston said, "Well, I guess good for him, but what does this have to do with us?"

"You told me about a treasure hunter named Lloyd Sinclair down in Jamaica. I thought maybe you could reach out to him and see if he wants to do some treasure hunting, but maybe on dry land by getting ahold of this stuff. My dad took a few pictures of the two items, and maybe you could pass them along to Mr. Sinclair to see what he thinks."

Fitzroy said, "Yeah, we could do that, but what's in it for us?"

"If he has any interest, and we find anything, I'm sure he would want to give you a piece. Plus, all I'm asking you to do is send an email and photo down to him. I'm not asking a lot."

Winston and Fitzroy looked at each other and smiled. Fitzroy said, "Yeah, we could do that, but I have to warn you that Mr. Sinclair doesn't like anyone wasting his time. Unless you're pretty sure that this might lead to something, it's not a good idea to get him involved."

"I'm confident that there's more to this than the guy was saying. He and a couple of other guys I know do a lot of treasure diving, and I really think that's where he got these pieces."

Winston said, "Okay, buy us a couple of more rounds, and we'll contact some people we know who can put us in touch with Mr. Sinclair. If he has any interest in these pieces and anything else, we'll let you know."

Bobby waved to the hostess and signaled for another round. Buying these two guys a couple of rounds of beer was a small price to pay to maybe hook into treasure. He smiled to himself, thinking about the beautiful dive shop he would have down in the islands.

Chapter Fourteen

The third day of our conference was shortened to a half-day. Most of the time was spent with the SEC talking about how they had been using stock and bond trading activity to uncover possible money laundering. I don't know if Sharon found it that interesting, but I was fascinated with how the SEC used computer models to determine possible illegal activities. It sounded like they had had a decent amount of success at catching banks that assisted in moving ill-gotten monies around the world.

After the SEC finished their presentation, we broke for a short lunch, and then a lot of the attendees got ready to head out. Sharon and I got to say goodbye to the FBI and CIA folks, and then we sat down with the SEC to talk about my possible involvement in the Public Company Accounting Oversight Board. Frank, George, and Linda joined Sharon and me to have coffee outside after lunch.

Frank began, "So, did the two of you enjoy our little conference?"

Sharon responded first with, "I thought it was great. As you know, it's not my bailiwick, but I really think I learned a lot. Plus, you never know when some of this stuff could help with a case. I've learned over the years, particularly from my adventures with Ben, that sometimes the biggest breaks can come from the strangest sources. Plus, everyone was super nice, which I have to admit surprised me some."

Linda said, "You figured we were all serious as hell federal law enforcement folks who couldn't be bothered to have some fun and a laugh now and then?"

"Sorry to say it, but that's exactly what I thought. But you folks are a lot of fun while also being very good at your jobs."

Frank said, "As the saying goes, take what you do seriously, but don't take yourself so seriously. Anyway, Ben, have you given any thought to joining the PCAOB?'

"I have. I'm still not entirely sure what I can add, and I'll admit that I'm a little nervous that I won't be able to run with the big dogs on this. I'm sure you've got some very talented people involved with PCAOB. Like I said when we first were talking about this, I'm just an accounting professor at a non-Ivy League school."

Linda jumped in with, "Ben, you are being too modest, which I have to admit is somewhat refreshing coming from an academic. Most of the profs we work with are so full of themselves that it's nauseating."

"So, how does it work? Do you send me things to look at, or are there meetings?"

George decided to jump in. "We'll be sending you documents to review, but there are also meetings. The meetings are normally at our headquarters in D.C., but sometimes we meet in New York. Rarely do we have to travel any farther than those two cities."

I inquired, "Ballpark, how much time do you expect me to spend each month?"

George replied, "Usually, our consultants spend about ten to twenty hours a month. As you can imagine, the workload increases during tax season but usually isn't too heavy during the fall. And we know you have a full-time job, so we know there are limits to how much time we can expect you to devote to the PCAOB."

Sharon smiled and asked, "Ben is too polite or gracious to ask, but I will: How much does it pay?"

Frank chuckled, "We had to get to that at some point. Normally we pay a consulting rate of $250 an hour."

Sharon looked at me, and I at her. She said, "Whoa, that's pretty decent pay. I think I may do some extra shopping while we are down here."

"Leave it to Sharon to have already spent the money before I've even earned it. Frank, that's a nice pay rate, but I have to admit that, at least early on, I don't know if my contributions will warrant that much money."

All three members of the SEC smiled. Linda said, "Ben, we picked you because we really think you can be helpful. And we weren't going to tell you this, but we talked to the chief of police in Philly. He told us that your consulting rate in Philly is about half of what we're offering, and you still do an excellent job for them. Ben, we have so many consultants who do little or nothing and still pick up a check. Don't worry, we're confident that we'll get our money's worth, and if not, we will tell you that we're not. One thing good about using consultants versus salaried people is that consultants usually have another source of income. That means they're not going to bleed you dry with their fees."

"Oh, I'll help Ben find a way to spend it," said Sharon.

"I'm sure you will," said Linda, "but that's between you and Ben. Anyway, Ben, should we send you a contract? Obviously, feel free to have your lawyer look it over."

I said, "Yes, I think I'm interested. To be totally frank, I'm pretty excited about it. I love teaching at Temple and doing a little work with Sharon for the Philly police, but this sounds like some fascinating stuff to be involved in. In fact, this may seem pompous, but I feel like this is something where I might really make a difference. Maybe help the accounting profession regain some credibility."

Frank put out his hand, "Then let's shake on a deal. We'll get the consulting contract emailed to you in the next few days."

I shook Frank's hand and then George and Linda's, too. "I look forward to working with all of you."

Linda said, "And we look forward to working with you. So, we're going to head out soon. What are you and Sharon going to do?"

"We extended our stay for a couple of days," I said. "We're going to do some sightseeing around here and then head down to Hatteras and Ocracoke. Since the weather is still pretty warm, we may try some kayaking over on the sound. Sharon wants to go hang-gliding, but that's a little shaky for me. Maybe, but maybe not."

Frank said, "Well, we all hope that you two have a great time, and again, we look forward to working with you on the PCAOB."

I thought that this trip turned out to be a great opportunity. And Sharon and I had finally taken a trip somewhere that didn't involve murder and drama.

Or at least that's what I thought!

Chapter Fifteen

Bobby Biltmore got a call from White and Reed that it was time for another meeting at Sam and Omie's. Bobby set it up for that afternoon.

White and Reed were already sitting at the bar when Bobby got there. Bobby got a beer, put the Jamaicans' beers on his tab, and adjourned to the deck outside to have some privacy.

Bobby said, "So you guys have some news?"

White said, "Yes, we do. Mr. Sinclair had an appraiser look at the pictures of the pieces you sent down. The appraiser said that it's a bit hard to tell exactly how old they are, but they are old. He thinks they might be from the golden age of piracy, so Mr. Sinclair is very interested. In fact, he is sending one of his best men, a Mr. Devon Ricketts, up here, and he'll arrive late tonight. Just so you know, Ricketts is very involved in Mr. Sinclair's illegal drug and smuggling businesses, so he is not one to fool around with. He's a serious guy, so I strongly encourage you to do what he says and when he says to do it."

"Ricketts is a mob guy?" said Bobby. "I thought Mr. Sinclair would send one of his divers or salvage guys up. I never thought he would send a mobster to try to get the loot."

Reed said, "What did you think would happen? We told you that Sinclair is a leading figure in the Jamaican mafia. When Sinclair needs something, he doesn't log on to Amazon. He has a member of his crew go get the stuff, whatever it may be. I'm a little surprised that Sinclair didn't come himself because he is fascinated with pirate treasure, but that's probably best for us. Sinclair tends to have little patience, and people get dead when he loses his patience. Ricketts is likely the same way, but he won't pull any guns or knives until he clears it with Sinclair. But, Bobby, I do hope that there's more loot to be found. The two pieces are nice, but Sinclair is no doubt looking for more."

Bobby just sat for a minute and couldn't help but be wondering to himself, "What the fuck have I gotten myself into? I was just looking for some extra dough to start a little dive business. Now I've got the Jamaican mob coming up to the little ole Outer Banks."

Bobby asked, "So when is Ricketts scheduled to get here?"

White replied, "He's flying into Norfolk, renting a car, and then coming straight down here. We are all supposed to meet him at his hotel, The First Colony Inn, at about 10 p.m."

Reed said, "Bobby, I'll repeat it, but I hope you understand that this guy is serious. He doesn't take no for an answer, and we better deliver something that he likes. You best be prepared that things might get a little ugly."

"What do you mean by ugly?"

"Well, I know that Ricketts has killed several of Mr. Sinclair's competitors in the drug business."

Bobby gulped and said, "Killed? As in murdered?"

Reed responded, "Yep, that's exactly what I mean. So, buckle in there, son. It might be a bumpy ride. But it could also be a very lucrative ride."

Bobby was already regretting this whole thing, but he knew it would be risky to try to halt it now. He was just going to have to suck it up and hope that no one got killed.

Especially him!

Chapter Sixteen

Bobby and his two new Jamaican partners sat quietly at the bar in the First Colony Inn. Bobby was scared as hell, but he could tell that his new buddies were really on edge, too. None of them had anything to say. They just sipped their drinks.

At about 10:30, a tall black man walked into the First Colony and came directly to the bar. He turned to Reed and said, "I'm Devon Ricketts. You guys the ones about the pirate treasure?"

Reed replied, "Yes, sir. That's us. My name is Fitzroy Reed, and this is Winston Whyte and Bobby Biltmore," as he introduced everyone.

Ricketts said, "Okay. Let me check in, and we'll go up to my room and talk. We don't need anyone overhearing our discussion."

With that, Ricketts went to the reservation desk and retrieved the key to his room. Then he returned to his rental car to get his suitcase. After that, he motioned for the three others to follow him up to his room.

The four of them went up to Ricketts's room on the third floor. It was hushed, indicating people were either asleep or there weren't that many guests. Ricketts opened his room door, and the four walked in. Ricketts pointed to a couch and chairs for the three guys to sit. Ricketts walked into the bedroom to stow his luggage and then came out.

He said, "So, gentlemen, we are going after pirate booty. Bring me up to speed on where things are."

Whyte decided to speak for the group. He said, "Well, sir, as you know, Bobby's dad owns a pawn shop. A young guy brought in two pieces to be examined. Bobby's dad is not an expert, but he thought both pieces were pretty old and might be worth something. He brought up the possibility that they might be pirate treasure. Bobby decided to involve us to see if there was a way for all of us to make some decent money on this. We contacted Mr. Sinclair, and he sent you up. That's about it."

Ricketts said, "So, Bobby, I heard from Mr. Sinclair that you had a feeling there might be more treasure than just the two pieces. What makes you think that?"

"Sir, I just had a feeling from watching the guy who brought it in. To be honest, I may be wrong, but I thought we might find out if there is more by contacting Winston and Fitzroy. At the least, we could find out if the story about the jewelry being inherited from his grandmother is true. Even if he doesn't have more treasure, we might be able to find out for sure where he got what he has."

Ricketts said, "Alright, I think I have the gist of it. What's the guy's name, and do you know where he lives?"

Bobby hesitated for a moment but said, "His name is Noah Spencer, and I know where his apartment is. Not far from here over in Manteo."

"Then here's the plan. This Spencer guy knows Bobby and may know the other two of you. So, we're going to take my rental over, and I'm going in to see Mr. Spencer. We'll have a discussion, and I'll find out quickly if there is any more treasure to be had. I can be very persuasive when I need to be."

Bobby, Fitzroy, and Whyte all took a deep breath. They didn't know what Ricketts would do, but it didn't sound enjoyable.

All four piled into Ricketts' car, and they headed over to Manteo. It only took them 30 minutes to find Spencer's apartment.

Ricketts said, "Okay, all three of you sit tight. I'll be back as soon as I find out if there is more treasure and if we can get our hands on it."

All three guys again sat quietly in Rickett's car. They were all nervous about what might happen. Finally, Winston said, "Okay, I'll say it for all of us: We may have made a mistake here. I'm worried that Ricketts might do Noah harm."

Bobby said, "No shit. Suppose Noah doesn't give this guy what he wants. Who knows what he might do? This sounded like a good idea when we started, but now it looks like a fuckup of historic proportions."

Fitzroy said, "Well, there sure as shit isn't anything we can do about it now. I just hope that your buddy Noah comes out okay."

After about 15 minutes, Ricketts returned to this car. He was carrying a burlap sack. He got into the car and started it up. At first, he didn't say anything that freaked the other three out. Finally, he said, "So things went very well. After a short little motivational speech, Spencer showed me where he had more treasure. He also told me that two of his friends have some booty stashed away. We're going to have to make the rounds to those houses, too."

Bobby sheepishly asked, "Motivational speech?"

"Yeah. Your pal is going to need to go to medical treatment to sew up his neck, but he'll be fine. And it was obvious that he should not involve the police or any other law enforcement. A small knife wound to the neck isn't that serious, but plenty of other things could be much more serious, perhaps deadly. I don't think we need to worry about him getting the cops involved. Go get some sleep and come back around lunch, and then we'll finish our work."

All three of them swallowed hard and also thought the exact same thing: This is turning out to be a very, very bad idea

.

Chapter Seventeen

While it was a chilly day, Sharon and I still decided to take a kayak trip out into the sound. We knew the ocean would be cold, but the sound didn't have many waves, so we figured we wouldn't get too wet. We found a store near the sound that sold kayak gear and other water sports equipment, and we rented two kayaks to take out in the sound. We got into our kayaks and headed out. As we thought, the water wasn't too choppy, and it was easy to move around.

Sharon said to me, "So what do you think? Are you having a good time?"

"I think it's fun, but I don't want to fall into the water. Looks pretty chilly."

"I agree. Let's just paddle around and see what we see."

As we moved away from shore, the beauty of the Outer Banks became apparent. We could see the other side of the sound and all the coastal houses that had been built. We looked down at the water and could see some small fish swimming around. As we moved farther from shore, we got a view of Jockey's Ridge and the sand dunes. In addition, we could see the Bodie Island Lighthouse. I had my phone wrapped in a plastic bag so it wouldn't get wet, but I could still take some pictures.

As we were making a turn, a small wave hit me; I tipped over some and scratched my arm on the underside of the kayak opening. At first, I thought it was just a scratch, and I didn't think anything of it. However, as we continued to paddle, I looked down and saw blood dripping down on the kayak. I took a towel, brushed away the dirt on my arm, and saw that the cut was pretty deep.

I paddled close to Sharon and said, "I think I may have a little problem."

"What's that?"

"I cut my arm on the kayak. It's bleeding a good bit."

"How could you cut yourself on the kayak? It's all plastic and has a smooth edge."

"There is a sharp edge on the underside of it, and I guess I pulled my arm across it and got cut."

Sharon said, "Do you think you need to get medical treatment?"

"Sorry, but I do think I need to have it looked at. It's probably nothing, but I think I should err on the side of caution. Can we return the kayaks and go over to the urgent care facility that we saw?"

"Of course. Don't want my guy to bleed out on me."

"I don't think I'm going to bleed out, but I might need a stitch or two."

"Then let's just paddle on in and get you looked at."

I took the towel I had and wrapped it around my arm. We headed in and turned in our kayaks. Sharon looked at it and agreed that it would be best to examine it. We headed over to the urgent care office we saw on Croatan Highway.

When we got there, we saw it wasn't that busy. Guess since it wasn't high season, it was pretty slow. I checked in at the front desk, and the nurse told me to have a seat.

I said to Sharon, "Sorry if I screwed up one of our days down here."

"Don't worry about it. It was an accident. The doc will give you a look-see, maybe do a stitch or two, and we'll continue enjoying our day. What do you want to do next?"

"I'm getting hungry. By the time this is finished, I'll probably be ready to eat. How about you?"

"I will probably be ready to eat, too. Got any idea of where you want to go?"

"Dirty Dick's Crab House is pretty close by. Wanna dig into some crabs?"

"They can be a lot of work for not that much food, but sure, let's give it a whirl."

Just then, a young man came out of the examining room. He had a good-sized bandage on his neck, but more than that, he looked scared to death. I said to Sharon, "Wonder how he hurt his neck like that?"

"No idea, but the kid looks very nervous. Wonder if it was a deep cut or something?"

'No idea, but, yeah, he looks very frightened. Maybe it just was a scary moment, and he's not over it yet. Do I look that terrified?"

"Nah, you just look like a guy who had a kayaking accident."

After the young man checked out, my name was called. I asked if Sharon could accompany me, and the nurse said yes.

Once in the examining room, the nurse said, "So, I'm Linda Boeing, and I'm here to do the first look at your cut. Can you remove the towel?"

I took off the towel, and Nurse Boeing took a look. She said, "So you did this on a kayak?"

I replied, "Yes, cut it on the underneath side of the kayak. At first, I didn't think it was that big a deal, but it kept bleeding, so I figured I should have it looked at."

"It is a pretty deep cut, and I think you might need three or four stitches. It will only take a minute, and then we can apply an antiseptic to prevent infection. I can do the stitching here, apply the ointment, and then let our doctor take a quick look. You can probably be out of here in 30 minutes or so."

Sharon said, "Thanks. We're headed out to Dirty Dick's to fight with some crabs."

"It's a great place, but you're right. It is a lot of work."

I said, "I know all about patient confidentiality, but that kid with the neck wound who was here before me looked terrified. Neck wound didn't look great, but we both thought the kid looked almost petrified."

"You're right, I'm not supposed to talk about other patients, but you're right that the kid was scared to death. His name is Noah, and he's from the area. He's been in for scrapes and the like several times. He's usually very talkative, but he barely said a word this time. When I asked him how it happened, he said he got it from working in his yard and was cut by a tree limb. It didn't look like a tree limb cut to me, looked like a knife wound, but it's not my place to say anything about it. Noah is in his early twenties, so I don't have any responsibility to report anything to the authorities. I just patched him up and sent him on his way. Anyway, let me go get the suture kit, and we'll get you patched up, too."

With that, the nurse left, and I turned to Sharon and said, "Maybe we should go file a report or something about that kid. It doesn't sound like his story holds up."

Sharon smiled and said, "No, Stone. We are not getting involved. If the nurse wasn't concerned enough to contact the authorities, then we are staying out of it, too. We will get you stitched up, and then we will wrestle with some crabs. We're not making this kid's accident our problem. We've been raising our hands too many times of late for things that are not our concern."

"You're right. The kid just cut himself on something and maybe is embarrassed that it happened. Not our problem."

It turns out we were wrong about that.

Chapter Eighteen

While Sharon and I had been kayaking and getting my cut sewed up, the Jamaican contingent plus Bobby were on the hunt for more treasure. Noah, under duress, had given out Jim's and Henry's apartment addresses. Ricketts decided that his entire group would go with him while he got the loot from the other guys.

Winston asked, "Mr. Ricketts, do you think it's a good idea to go to these houses during the daylight? People might see you going in."

Ricketts replied, "I don't care. Once I retrieve the treasure from these two chumps, I'll be leaving this god-forsaken place and heading back to the beauty of Jamaica."

"But, sir, how do we know if they're home or not? Maybe they are at their jobs," asked Bobby.

"Nah, that kid Noah told me that they had taken some time off as they tried to figure out what to do with all the loot. As I said, I can be very persuasive when I need to be."

As they approached Jim's home, Ricketts said, "The three of you just stay in the car. I'll go up and see if anyone is home, particularly the kid with the treasure. I will discuss why he should hand it over if he's here. It certainly worked with the first kid, so I'm confident I can convince him to cooperate. If someone else is also there, we can come back tonight."

Ricketts parked on the street next to Jim's apartment. The other three sat in the car as instructed while Ricketts went up to the door. He rang the doorbell, but there was no answer. He rang the doorbell next door, and an older woman came to the door. The three in the car could see that Ricketts was talking to her. After only a few minutes, he returned to the car.

He threw the door open and cursed, "Shit. That little bastard."

Winston asked, "What happened, sir?   He wasn't home?"

"No, he wasn't home, and according to his neighbor, he hasn't been home all day. I think the first guy tipped him off, and he went into hiding."

Bobby said, "But I thought you said that Noah said he would cooperate and not tell the cops."

"He probably didn't tell the cops, but he told at least one of his partners. We're going to go see the other one, and if he's also in hiding, then we may have to go back to the first guy and have another motivational speech."

Bobby, Winston, and Fitzroy all looked at each other and shuddered. This whole thing was getting worse and worse.

The four found their way to Henry's house and got the same answer from a neighbor. Henry hasn't been around.

Once again, Ricketts returned to the car and was now even more pissed than before. He turned to the three and said, "Okay, boys, we're heading back to the first guy's apartment. I'm sure he'll know where the other two are."

They drove back to Noah's apartment. Ricketts went to the door and hit the alarm. No one answered. He went back to the car.

"Okay, boys, he's not answering. Who knows where he might be?"

All three guys shook their heads. Bobby said, "I haven't seen him in years until he came in with the two pieces of treasure. I have no idea where he might hang out these days other than his apartment."

Ricketts said, "So who knows what his cell phone number might be?"

Again, all three shook their heads. They had no idea what his cell phone might be.

Ricketts asked, "Okay, Bobby, do you know where he lived when he was growing up. Maybe his family still lives there."

Bobby shook his head and said, "Noah and I weren't very close, so I don't know where he grew up."

Ricketts took a good look at Bobby's face, unsheathed his knife, and put it to Bobby's neck. "I don't believe you. I think you know where he used to live. In fact, I'm willing to run this knife over your throat to find out."

Bobby didn't know what to do. He did know where Noah grew up, but he didn't want to tell Ricketts about it. He tried to bluff some more. "Really, I haven't seen Noah in years. As I said, we were never that close."

Ricketts took the knife and pressed it against Bobby's neck. He took a small slice across his carotid artery, just enough to draw some blood. He said, "If I don't hear someplace to go look for this guy in the next ten seconds, there is going to be a lot more blood in this car."

Bobby caved and, with a shaky voice, said, "His family used to have a small cabin over on the other side of the sound near Wanchese. We went there a few times when we were young to fish. I don't even know if it's even still there or if they still own it, but it's a place where he might hide." Bobby felt instantly guilty about giving up the place.

Ricketts took the knife off Bobby's neck and said, "See. That wasn't that hard. You sit upfront and give me directions to this place."

The four headed off to Wanchese with the other two Jamaicans sitting in the back. Much had changed since Bobby had last been there, but with Ricketts providing motivation with the knife, Bobby eventually tracked down the small cabin.

Ricketts said, "All three of you stay in the car. I'm taking the keys, so you can't drive away, and if you run, I will find you, and I will kill you. Understand?"

All three nodded, and Ricketts got out of the car. He made his way up to the cabin. He looked in the window and saw there was a light on. He went up to the door, took a short running start, and slammed his shoulder into the door. It gave way quickly, and he went in.

The three in the car were trying to figure out how to escape, but they were all fearful that Ricketts would make good on his threat. As much as they wanted to run, they sat almost paralyzed in the car.

After about twenty minutes, Ricketts exited the cabin. He leaned into the car and said, "Okay, you two Jamaicans go get a tarp or a sheet. Go get the body in the cabin, and I'll open the trunk, and you'll put the covered body in the trunk. Then we're going over to the causeway and dump the body into the sound."

Bobby screamed, "You killed him? Why?"

"Yes, I did, and if you don't keep your voice down, you will join him. Mr. Sinclair and I don't like loose ends, and this guy was one. But his death was not a waste. I got his cell phone and found the numbers of the other two treasure hunters. I've already called them, and, not surprisingly, neither picked up. But that's okay because after we dump this body, I will call again and leave them an important message."

Winston stammered some and said, "What message are you going to leave?"

"That I'm going to start killing you three, one at a time, until they give up the treasure."

Chapter Nineteen

Sharon and I woke up at about 9. We put on some clothes and made some coffee in the coffee maker in our room.

Sharon asked, "So, how is your arm today?"

"It's fine. It stings a little bit, but it's all good. Any idea on what you want to do today?"

"Not sure. You're the one who's injured, so what do you want to do?"

I said, "Injury is no big deal. I feel a little cheated on our tour of the sound and maybe even the ocean. Any interest in going back out to the water?"

"Sounds great. Probably need to skip the kayak, though. Too cold to water ski or jet ski. How about we rent a tiny boat and do a couple of laps around the sound?"

"Works for me. Let me make a call to see if there is something available."

I called around to a few boating stores. It seemed that most of the stores only had kayaks and jet skis. Finally, I found one with a small sailboat that held only two or three people. Sounded perfect for us.

We dressed in some warm clothes and took the short trip over to the boating store. It was right next to the sound. The owner showed us the sailboat and gave us a quick tutorial on maneuvering it. We had done a little sailing on the New Jersey shore, so we weren't wholly novices, but it had been a while. Since the wind wasn't blowing that hard, the owner told us we should be fine just cruising around the sound.

We rented the boat, got the sail set up, and pushed off into the sound. I got us adequately adjusted with the sail, and before long, we were cruising around the sound, although not very quickly.

I asked, "So what do you think?"

"It's great, Stone. You're better at this sailing thing than I thought you would be. We're not moving quickly, but we're getting around very steady. And there is a lot to look at. Did you bring your camera in the plastic bag?"

"I did indeed, and I'll get some shots of the sound and water as we sail around."

As we were cruising around, I took several shots. Like before, we saw a lot of birds flying by and even the occasional fish in the water. I decided to get us a little closer to the land to see any wildlife I could photograph.

As we got closer to land, I saw what looked like a mound that had been washed ashore. I got a little closer to it and said to Sharon, "Do you see that? What does it look like to you?"

"I can't tell from here, but it looks like it might be some sort of aquatic life that washed ashore. Why don't we get closer?"

I maneuvered us closer to the mound on the sand, and as we approached, we both gasped. Sharon was the first to say, "I think that looks like a body! What do you think?"

"I hate to say it, but, yeah, it looks like a body to me, too. We need to get closer."

I aimed us at the object lying on the sand and got us close enough that I could run the sailboat aground so we could see what it was. Once we were close to the edge of the beach, we both got out of the water and pulled the sailboat closer to shore to make sure it didn't drift away while we got out.

We walked over to the object and immediately could tell it was a body. It was turned over on its stomach so that we couldn't see any of its features.

I asked, "Shit, what should we do?"

Sharon replied, "Well, according to the protocol, we should leave it alone and not disturb the crime scene, but I want to see the face to make sure he's really dead, so I think we should gently turn the body over. It won't alter the crime scene that much."

We turned the body over and were shocked once again. Sharon said, "He's dead, and isn't this the kid we saw at urgent care?"

"It is, and I know that for sure because this body has the same neck injury that the kid at urgent care had, plus a deep slit across his neck. What the fuck is going on here?"

"I have no idea, but we need to call 911 on your phone to get the police over here. We'll stick around till they get here so we can give a statement."

I called 911 and was immediately patched through to the operator. The operator said, "911, what is your emergency?"

"Hello, we are tourists here who were out sailing this morning. While we were sailing, we found a body that had washed ashore. We pulled our sailboat aground, got out and saw the body up close, and then called you."

"Can you give me an idea of where you are? Are there any signs or identifying landmarks that the police can use to find you?"

"There is a water tower that says Kill Devil Hills that is almost directly in front of us. Does that give you any idea where we are?"

"Actually, it does. I will contact our police department and get them to you as soon as possible. It should be pretty quick. Naturally, please don't leave the area as the police will want to talk to you."

I said, "Of course, we'll stay right here."

While we waited for the police, I asked Sharon, "So what do you think happened?"

"Well, obviously, it looks like the cause of death was a knife wound cut across his neck, although maybe he drowned before he bled out. Hard to say for sure, but it looks like he bled out before he went into the water. The ME will be able to tell more."

After only a few minutes, we heard sirens coming closer to us, and in just a moment, we saw the flashing lights from two police cars come around the corner. They pulled right up to where we were standing, and both officers exited their vehicles.

The first one, a tall Black man, said, "Stay right there. Don't move."

Sharon whispered to me, "Just play along. They probably don't get much of this kind of stuff down here. They're probably going to overreact a little. Seen too many cop shows."

The other cop was white, and he stood close to Sharon and me and had his hand on his revolver. Way too many cop shows.

Sharon said, "Officers, we are the ones who called 911, so it's a pretty good bet that we didn't hurt this guy. My name is Sharon Levin, and I'm a homicide cop in Philadelphia for what it's worth. My friend here is Dr. Ben Stone, a professor at Temple University."

Both cops seemed to calm down a bit, and the white guy said, "My name is Bill Brown, and my partner here is Fred Jones. So, tell us what happened here."

Sharon replied, "Ben and I were out doing a little sailing on the sound, and we saw this mound from probably a half-mile or so away. We couldn't tell what it was from out there, so we came closer, and, as we got closer, we could see it was a human body. We got our sailboat close to the sandbar and pulled it onto the beach so it wouldn't float away. We got out of the sailboat, came closer, saw the body, and immediately called 911."

Brown asked, "Did you touch the body?"

"Yes, it was on its stomach when we got here, and I rolled it over just to check for vitals. We were pretty sure he was dead, but I just wanted to be sure. I've been a homicide cop for many years, and strange things can happen. But other than rolling the body a half-turn, we've not touched it."

Brown nodded, and Jones took their first good look at the body. Jones said, "Shit, this is Noah Spencer. I know his parents. He's from the area."

Brown said, "I know him too because he used to play soccer with my son in high school. I've seen him around occasionally, but not in a while. I heard he has, or had, an apartment over near Manteo. I had heard that he was doing quite well."

"Well, he's not doing very well right now. Look at that knife wound. Someone was pretty serious about making sure that Noah was killed. I can't imagine how this could happen. He was a good kid. Never got into any trouble or at least none that I know about."

Jones said, "Same here. He always was a good guy. Well-liked. Went off to East Carolina, as I recall. Should have finished up a couple of years ago. Anyway, we need to call the medical examiner and get his body moved."

Jones said to Sharon and me, "So I know you two are probably on vacation, but we're going to need a statement from you. It shouldn't take long. It's pretty obvious that you had nothing to do with what happened to Noah."

Sharon snickered and said, "Thanks for the vote of confidence. Yeah, we know how it works with statements. We have about 90 minutes or so left on our sailing adventure. Okay, if we come in for that statement after that?"

Brown said, "Sure. We won't hear anything from the ME for a while. Take your time. We're not going anywhere. Sorry to screw up your vacation."

I said, "Well, first off, sorry about this kid getting killed as it sounds like he was a pretty decent guy. As far as screwing up our vacation, we've had much bigger things happen on vacation than only having to make a statement at the police station. No problem."

Little did we realize that our vacation was getting ready to get much more complicated and very soon!

Chapter Twenty

Ricketts had told Bobby, Winston, and Fitzroy to meet him at a pancake house at 8 a.m. None of the three had slept a wink that night and had discussed how they might flee. However, all three felt that Ricketts seemed so relentless in getting what he wanted that he would somehow track them down if they escaped. And even if he didn't, they would always be looking over their shoulders for fear that he would. They didn't like any of their options, but all three felt that going along with Ricketts was their best chance of survival, so they all showed up at the pancake house at the appointed time,

Ricketts was waiting for them when they arrived. He said, "Have a seat, boys. Get some coffee and something to eat. We are going to have a busy day."

None of the three were hungry, but they all got coffee. Bobby was the first to ask, "So, sir, what do we have to do today."

"Well, I have some good news and maybe also some bad. Mr. Sinclair has taken a personal interest in this treasure hunt, and he is on his way up here on his private jet. In fact, he should be here in about two hours. He's landing at the Dare County Regional Airport so he will be close by. Once he is here, we will figure out our next moves. But I will tell you that since Mr. Sinclair is coming up here personally, we better find some of the treasure we've been hunting for. Mr. Sinclair is even less patient than I am, so you guys might want to spend the next couple of hours coming up with a sure-fire means of getting the extra loot."

All three looked at each other and swallowed hard. Having Sinclair come in was only going to up the stakes for success, and all three knew that failure was not an option or certainly an option they did not want to test.

Winston inquired, "We know you left a voice message about what you were going to do if you didn't hear from them. Have you heard anything?"

"No, not yet. They may not be checking their voice mail. In fact, you three should hope that they're not since my voice mail said I was going to start killing you three if they didn't respond. If they heard that message and are choosing to ignore it, I guess they're not your friends."

Bobby said, "I wouldn't call them friends, but I would hope they would want to help if they knew about the threat. I'm going to believe that they didn't, for whatever reason, know about the threat."

Ricketts smiled and said, "Doesn't really matter. Mr. Sinclair has decided to keep you guys around for the time being. Since we don't know for sure if the other treasure hunters got my message, we don't know if it would be helpful to kill one of you. For your information, Mr. Sinclair has no problem killing or having people killed, but there has to be a reason and a payoff for doing so. Right now, we don't have one for you three. So at least for now, you three are off the hook."

All three took a deep breath and leaned back a little. Fitzroy inquired, "So what should we do until Mr. Sinclair arrives?"

"Well, I guess you two Jamaicans can tell me how you ended up in this godforsaken place. This place sucks compared to Jamaica, so what the hell are you doing here?"

Winston said, "We both love Jamaica, but we were having a hard time finding work. We didn't know anyone in the government, so many doors were closed to us. We knew that we wanted to fish for at least a couple of years, but there was just too much competition down in Jamaica. We had heard about fishing up here, so we decided to come up and try it for a while."

"So was it a good idea, or were you stupid as hell? I'm guessing stupid as hell."

"Actually, it has been great," said Fitzroy. "We found a couple of boats we can crew on regularly. We've made good money, and the cost of living here is pretty low. We've been able to put away some dough so we can return to Jamaica and have our own boat."

Ricketts smiled and said, "Maybe you could have found work with Mr. Sinclair. He pays a lot better than working on a fishing boat."

Neither Winston nor Fitzroy wanted to take a chance of insulting Ricketts, so they said nothing. Ricketts grinned, "Yeah, that would probably have been a bad idea. You two don't look like drug runners to me. You'd probably get killed on your first voyage. Probably better that you stayed up here and fished some. How about you, Bobby? What did you want to be when you grow up?"

"You know that I've been working at my dad's pawn shop. He's made a pretty decent living over the years with it, and I've been learning the business. All the new online shopping has impacted our profits, but my dad recently paid a computer nerd to develop a website where we can post the things that come into the store. We've developed a decent online presence yet, and the website is starting to get more traffic, so we think things are looking up."

Ricketts laughed and said, "And now all three of you are hooked with the Jamaican mob. Guess you didn't see that coming. By the way, you should know that Mr. Sinclair is very generous to those people who deliver what he wants. If you three can help him get the rest of the treasure, I'm sure he'll compensate you well. Anyway, gentlemen, have another cup of coffee, and then we'll head over to the airfield. I'm sure Mr. Sinclair is anxious to arrive and get started on our treasure hunt.

None of the three believed him for a second about the compensation, and none of them really cared anymore about getting paid by a Jamaican mobster. Mostly they just wanted to come out of this whole thing still alive. And they all knew that if they didn't find some more treasure, the likelihood of that happening was looking pretty dim.

Chapter Twenty-One

After we finished our boating time, we showered and changed and took a trip to the Nags Head Police Department. It was a short drive to the headquarters. Officers Brown and Jones were waiting for us.

Jones said, "Thanks for coming by so quickly. It won't take that long. Can I get you a coffee or something?"

I said, "I'm fine." Sharon nodded that she was also okay. The officers took us back to an office with chairs and a table.

Jones said, "So we already know some of what happened, but could you give us the details again?"

"Since Sharon is a cop, I'll let her do the talking."

Sharon grinned and said, "Probably just as well since Ben is a professor and tends to ramble on. Anyway, we went out yesterday to do some kayaking. We were having a great time, but then Ben got the cut, you see, on his arm. It didn't seem like a big deal, but we decided to look it over at urgent care. That's when we first saw the victim. He was getting his neck bandaged up while we were waiting. Didn't really think anything of it at the time. Today, we decided to go back out for a little while, renting a small sailboat. We were sailing around the sound when we saw this object over by the sand. We couldn't tell what it was until we got closer and realized it was a body. We took our sailboat, grounded it on the sandbar, and went over to see the situation. As I told you, the kid's body was turned over with his face and stomach facing down. I was pretty sure he was already gone, but I did turn him over to check for vitals. Confirmed he was dead, and we called 911, and you guys came."

Brown inquired, "When you saw Noah at urgent care, did anything seem out of place?"

"We only saw him for a minute," said Sharon, "but we both thought he looked pretty nervous. The cut was a little deep, but his anxiety or fear seemed well beyond what it should be. We didn't know the kid, so we really didn't think much about it. But naturally, we were surprised when we found the body on the beach over on the sound."

Brown asked, "See anybody else out while you were boating?"

I said, "No one close by. We saw a couple of windsurfers out, but they were at least half to a full mile from us. And they were surfing around the whole time we were out, so it's hard to imagine that they had anything to do with this. They certainly weren't in a hurry to leave."

Jones said, "Did you see anything floating near or around him when you first came up?"

Sharon replied, "Nope, just the body. Didn't see anything in the water or on the sand. I didn't even see tire tracks in the sand leading into where the kid was dumped. I don't know if the culprits cleaned up or the sand and surf going in and out just washed away any evidence. Sorry, guys. I know from experience that any clues can be helpful, but I don't think I have anything to add. Do you, Ben?"

"Nope, that's pretty much all I have, too. Naturally, if we think of anything that might be helpful, we'll be in touch."

Jones said, "That would be helpful. Thanks."

"So, since I'm a cop, I have to ask, you got any leads or ideas on why this happened?"

"It's early, but right now, it's not looking that promising. Noah has lived here most of his life. He went away to college but came back once he graduated. He has never been in any serious trouble. He had a couple of parties at his apartment that got a little loud, and we had to tell them to keep it down, but other than that, he's always been a perfect kid. We don't think he had a girlfriend right now, but I'm pretty sure he's had them over the years. My point is that he wasn't some sort of weirdo into strange things, or at least we don't think he was. We only know that he had a couple of buddies with whom he did a lot of scuba diving, looking for pirate treasure. I don't think they had any luck, but they were very determined. Went out a lot down by Ocracoke Island. Even had wet suits to go out when the water was cold. But I will say that we have a lot of treasure hunters around here, with all the Blackbeard lore and such. Plus, they found some of Blackbeard's ship, *The Queen Anne's Revenge*, a few years back. It was nothing that valuable, cannonballs and the like, but it set off a storm of people searching for treasure. It's slowed down some since then, but hope springs eternal when it comes to treasure."

I asked, "So what's the next step?"

Jones replied, "Well, the first thing is the worst thing we have to do. We have to tell his parents that he's gone. Sharon, you've probably done this a few times, but it's unusual down here. In fact, neither of us has had to do a death notice before. We don't even know what to say."

"There's no easy way," said Sharon. "About all you can do, tell them and then let them cry their eyes out, which is absolutely going to happen. Both parents will lose it, and all you can do is be there for them and maybe say some kind words about the kid. And, of course, tell them that you will do everything possible to find the killer or killers. That usually helps some even if you don't know if you are likely to have any luck on finding the culprits."

"Thanks, that helps," said Brown. "Anyway, I guess that's all we need right now. Thanks again for coming in."

Sharon and I shook hands with the cops, and we left. When we got into the car, I said to Sharon, "You're going to try to get involved in this, aren't you?"

"No way. I feel sorry for them and naturally for the kid and his family, but this is not our problem, and I'm not going to make it ours."

I leaned over and put my hand on her shoulder and said, "I don't believe you, but maybe you will prove me wrong."

She didn't!

Chapter Twenty-Two

Bobby, Winston, Fitzroy, and the scary Mr. Ricketts got to the small Outer Banks local airport before Sinclair's arrival time. They saw a limo waiting close to the airstrip when they got there. According to information Ricketts got via a satellite phone, Sinclair was about 15 minutes away. The four of them just sat silently in Ricketts' car. The three youngsters had absolutely nothing they wanted to say, so if Ricketts was happy with quiet, so were they.

As they sat in the car, they could hear a plane approaching. Bobby knew that the airport was not tended, no air controller, radar, or any of the like. It was just up to the pilot to land the damned thing. They all four looked up simultaneously and saw a very sleek corporate jet headed their way. It was the nicest jet Bobby had ever seen.

The jet was making its approach to the airstrip. It sat down very smoothly and stopped not far from the car. The pilot throttled back all the power on the plane, and it got quiet. The door opened, and a small ladder was extended down to the tarmac. All four guys in the car were standing, and the head of the Jamaican mob came down the steps.

Bobby was a bit surprised. He had expected Sinclair to be a frightening fellow just like Ricketts, but he wasn't. In fact, he looked more like a teacher, professor, or just legitimate businessman than he did a mob boss. He wasn't wearing very flashy clothes. Didn't have tons of jewelry on. The only thing he had that stood out a bit was he was wearing a fedora, but even that wasn't that flashy. Just a nice hat. He looked to Bobby more like an uncle than a killer. But from what Ricketts had said, this guy was dangerous.

Sinclair reached the bottom of the ladder and walked over to shake hands with Ricketts. They even had a bit of a man hug. Ricketts said, "Welcome to the Outer Banks, Mr. Sinclair." He then turned and said, "Mr. Sinclair, these are the three guys who are going to find the treasure for us. Their names are Bobby, Winston, and Fitzroy."

Sinclair didn't offer a hand. He said, "So two of you young fellas are from Jamaica. I don't know why the fuck you would come here versus Jamaica, but why do I care." He turned to Ricketts and said, "So where are we on finding the loot?"

"Sir, why don't we go get you checked into your room, and I'll bring you up to speed on my plan."

"You can tell me about your plan on the way to my room. I don't want to spend any more time in this cold-ass place than I have to. I have two drivers in the limo. You can sit with me, Ricketts, and the other driver will bring these three little punks along to my hotel. And I hope you have some good news about finding the money. I have a lot of obligations down in Jamaica, and while I really want this treasure, I have no interest in turning this into a quest. Get the loot and get the hell out of here."

"Of course, Mr. Sinclair. I'm happy to ride with you and update you on our progress. You are also in The First Colony Inn?"

"Yes. Let's get going."

Sinclair and Ricketts got into the limo while the second driver took over Ricketts's car. Bobby, Winston, and Fitzroy just sat in silence. They did not introduce themselves, and the driver just stayed quiet.

Sinclair had the limo driver close the window between the front row of the limo and the back so the driver could not hear their conversation. He said, "So, where is this supposed treasure trove of jewelry and gold?"

"Right now, we don't know, sir. We know the two other guys who have part of the treasure, but we don't know where they are now. They have gone into hiding. I got the cell phone from the one I killed and left a threatening voice mail for them. I told them that either they give up the loot, or I would start killing these three."

"Have you heard anything yet?"

"No, sir. I'm going on the assumption that they heard the voice mail, but maybe not. I would think that the threat would make them contact me about how to get the valuables to prevent a death, but they have not contacted me so far. An explanation would be that they didn't listen to the voice mail."

"So, if they don't contact you, how are you going to track them down?"

Ricketts replied, "That's where those three come in. The kid named Bobby knows the two who are in hiding and can help us track them down. The two Jamaicans know their way around this area, but Bobby has lived here his entire life, so he's very well-versed in the surrounding area. I'm sure he can find some likely places the two with the jewels might hide."

"Ricketts, I have to say that I'm a little underwhelmed. It sounds like you plan to have three little jerkoffs comb these islands, hoping to find out and find where the two are hiding. The place isn't that big, but I assume there are a lot of places to hide out, and they may not even be in this area anymore. They may have hightailed it out of here and gone who knows where. This could take a long time to track them down and get the loot. I thought you were further along than that."

"Sir, I really thought the threatening phone call would rattle them enough to get them to come out and exchange the jewels for keeping these three alive. I'll call them again and increase the threat level. Tell them I'll track down their families if necessary to get their cooperation."

"Okay, I don't want to involve their families unless it's vital. It's not that I'm not willing to, but it should be a last resort. You may not believe it, but even I have a heart, and I don't want to involve innocent parents. But, if we have to, we will. What I want you to do is get those three morons looking for the two with the loot. And feel free to threaten them if need be."

"Brilliant idea, Mr. Sinclair. I'll get the ball rolling on this plan as soon as we get you settled. I feel confident that we can get you what you want."

"Ricketts, you don't need to kiss my ass. Just get me the fucking loot. And by the way, what do you plan to do with those three once we get what we need?"

"Maybe dispose of them, but we may not need to. Once we have the jewels, you and I will be heading back to the island. There's nothing these three can tell the authorities that will impact us. We'll be in the clear, and you'll have what you want."

"You better be right. I have no problem having those three killed, and just so you know, having you eliminated would also not cost me one night of sleep. So, you better deliver."

For the first time, Ricketts himself had to swallow hard. He wasn't used to being scared, he was usually the one scaring, but even he had to choke a bit on Sinclair's words. Stakes were going up, and he couldn't afford to be unsuccessful. Time to find some treasure.

Chapter Twenty-Three

While Sharon and I were trying to decide how to spend our last couple of days down in N.C., Bobby and the Jamaican contingent were deciding how to proceed. But the most important happening was down at the end of Hatteras Island because that's where Jim and Henry were hiding out.

When Jim got the call from Noah about Sinclair attacking him over the treasure, both Jim and Henry felt they had to hide. Given what happened to Noah, they were more than willing to give up the treasure they had on hand. They would still have the loot they had stored at Jim's parents' home. But they had heard that Jamaicans, in general, were ruthless, so they didn't feel they could trust the Jamaicans to take the money and leave them alone. They knew they didn't have a plan, but they were sure they needed to find a place to hide.

At first, they felt that heading inland would be best. Head toward central North Carolina and away from the Outer Banks. But they decided that they knew better where to hide if they stayed around the Outer Banks. They had both lived their lives there, so they knew several places where they could hide.

They decided to head down to Cape Hatteras. They needed to get away from where the Jamaican action was happening. Plus, they already knew of a small house over by the sound that was not visible from the road that they could rent. They called the real estate company and rented the small place for a week with the understanding they might stay longer. They found a small food store where they stocked up on some provisions. Once they had enough food for a few days, they hunkered down in their little abode. There was no reason to spend too much time out in public if someone recognized them. That was unlikely, but why take the chance?

At first, they thought they would call their parents and let them know they would be out of touch for a while. But they decided that phoning might be risky if somehow the Jamaicans had access to tracking phone calls. They both thought they were being very paranoid, it was unlikely the Jamaicans had such electronic surveillance ability, but it was better to err on the side of caution. They emailed their parents, telling them they were taking some time off from work to do some fishing. It was a weak excuse, but they didn't want their parents involved in all this intrigue. Their parents had emailed back and just told them to be careful. Told them to be in touch.

Jim made them some eggs, sausage, and toast. They gathered in the kitchen and sat down to eat. They were both hungry, but they knew they needed to figure out their next steps. Food was important, but so was staying alive.

Jim said, "Well, we can hole up here for a while. It would be hard for anyone to find us. But what the fuck are we going to do to try to get out of this? You got any good ideas?"

Henry replied, "I wish I did. Sure, we would be happy to give up our separate pieces of the treasure to the Jamaicans, particularly since we have a chunk of it stored at your house. But I don't know how we can get it to them without risking them finding out where we are."

"Maybe Noah could get a message to the Jamaicans for us?"

"I've tried emailing Noah, but I haven't heard from him. Maybe we should just call him?"

Jim said, "I decided to give that a try yesterday. His cell phone was dead. I tried again today, and the same results. Phone was dead."

"That's weird," said Henry. "Noah always has his phone with him and charged. Do you think something happened to him?"

Jim replied, "I hope not, but these Jamaicans are ruthless. Think we should try his family to see if he's okay?"

"Yeah, it's worth a try. I know we shouldn't use phones, just email, but we don't have his family's email address. We can look up his family's phone number in the online phone directory. I'm worried, and I think we need some assurances that he's okay."

Henry went to the online phone directory and found Noah's family's landline number. He dialed it on his cell phone. The phone rang many times, and Henry was ready to hang up when there was an answer suddenly. Jim couldn't tell who Henry was talking to, but he could see that Henry's face quickly turned white, and he lost all color. Jim could even notice that Henry's hands were now shaking. He spoke to whoever was on the phone for just a few more minutes. Then he hung up and just flopped down on the sofa. Jim sat next to him but didn't say anything.

Finally, Henry said, "Noah is dead."

"What the fuck do you mean Noah is dead?"

"His throat was slit, and his body dumped in the sound. Some tourists found him yesterday. The funeral is scheduled for tomorrow. I spoke to one of his distant cousins. His close family is too upset to take any phone calls."

Jim just sat for a moment with his head in his hands. Finally, he said, "It was a Jamaican, right?"

"Had to be. Obviously, it was not an accident."

"Well, we have to go to his funeral, right?" asked Jim.

"Are you nuts? I feel awful about Noah, but we can't be seen anywhere near his funeral. If that Jamaican sees us, we'll be joining Noah in an early grave."

"But Noah is our best friend, and we apparently helped get him killed with this treasure hunt."

Henry said, "I know. I can't believe I'm saying we shouldn't go, but it's not going to make Noah's family feel better if we get killed, too."

"So, what do you think we should do?" inquired Jim.

"I have no real idea right now. Maybe we should just turn ourselves into the police, give them all the loot, including what's in your family's basement, and let them sort out what to do with it."

At first, Jim thought that might work, but then he reconsidered. "At first glance, that sounds great, but what happens if it just pisses off the Jamaicans and they come after us? They will be outraged if they don't feel like they got most of the booty. I'm not ready to spend the rest of my life in the Witness Protection Program."

"So, we're just going to have to figure out a way to get them what they want without getting ourselves killed."

Henry made that sound a lot easier than it was going to be.

Chapter Twenty-Four

Sharon and I got up early to figure out what we wanted to do for our last couple of days at the Outer Banks. We showered, got dressed, and headed out to a pancake house.

Once we had ordered and were waiting for our food, I asked, "So what strikes your fancy for these last couple of days?"

Sharon gave me the look. I knew all too well what the look meant. I asked, "You want to get involved in finding out what happened to the kid we found in the sound, don't you?"

She smiled and said, "You know me all too well. I know we should just leave it alone. It's not our problem, and it's unlikely that we'll find something that the local cops won't find. We don't know our way around this area, we have no resources, and we're unlikely to uncover something the local cops won't find. It would likely be a total waste of our time to pursue this."

"But you want to do it anyway."

"I'm sorry, Ben. I know I sort of promised that we would stay out of this, but the cop in me makes that hard. Finding that kid unceremoniously dumped in the sound and washed up on land pisses me off. I'm sure his parents are grieving and will be for a while. I just can't get that vision out of my head. I want to do something, but I admit that I don't even know where to start. What do you think we should do?"

"I know you well enough to know that if we don't do something, this will gnaw at you for a while. How about we devote today to trying to do a little sleuthing about what happened? You're right, we probably won't find out much, but I think you will feel better if we at least put a little time into trying. Does that work for you?"

"You are more than fair, but I still don't know where to start. We could go back to the local cops and offer to help, but I'm not sure they'll be receptive to our assistance. Might come across as a homicide cop from the big city of Philadelphia trying to throw her weight around to help the poor little hick cops from the Outer Banks."

I said, "I have an idea." I signal for our waitress to come back, and I say that we would like a refill on our coffee. When she returned with our coffee, I asked, "So we're only here for a couple of more days, but we want to get some of the local flavors of the area, not just the tourist stuff. Can you direct us to a place where the locals hang out?"

The waitress said, "A lot of locals go to the Jolly Roger for food. Owens Restaurant is also trendy. If you're looking for drinks, Sam and Omie's is the place to go."

Sharon asked, "So Sam and Omie's is where locals go to crack a beer?"

"Absolutely. Sam and Omie's has been here forever and is a trendy haunt for the locals."

I said, "That sounds perfect. I saw the place as we were driving around. It's down close to the causeway, isn't it?"

"Right there before you go over the causeway or head down the Hatteras Island. Can't miss it."

I thanked the waitress, asked for our check, left a very generous tip, and we headed out. It only took us a few minutes to get down to Sam and Omie's from the pancake house.

We went in and decided to sit at the bar figuring the bartender might be willing to chat us up some. We ordered two draft beers and just sat talking about the weather, the Eagles, and how much fun we thought the Outer Banks was.

After a few minutes, the bartender returned to see if we needed a beer refill or food. I said, "No, I think we're fine right now. However, we're staying up at the First Colony and heard a story that some kid washed up on shore on the good side. Sounds pretty gruesome."

The bartender said, "It's just awful. The kid's name is Noah Spencer, and he was a local. Good kid. Never got into any trouble that I know of. Had a decent job, apartment over in Manteo, and just did a lot of diving with a couple of buddies of his."

"He did a lot of diving?" asked Sharon. "What was he diving for?"

"Same thing as everyone around here: sunken treasure. People have been chasing pirate treasure for hundreds of years around here. No one has had much luck, but I did hear a rumor that Noah and his buddies may have made a score. Probably just another Outer Banks rumor, but a couple of folks have been in here saying they had heard that Noah and his buddies, two guys named Jim Norman and Henry Riddick, may have found something. I heard Noah took a couple of jewelry pieces into a pawn shop to get them appraised. He said he found them in his grandmother's jewelry, but that story seemed a little thin. Apparently, the jewelry was worth a good bit of money, and Noah's grandmother was far from wealthy."

"Think that might have anything to do with his death?" inquired Sharon.

"Hard for me to say. I don't even know if the cops know about the pawnshop. Maybe I should call the cops and tell them about the pawnshop and the jewelry just in case they don't know about it."

I said, "It certainly wouldn't do any harm to let them know. You should give them a heads up. Anyway, can I get our check? We need to head out to do some sightseeing."

The bartender brought me our check, again I tipped generously, and we headed back to our car. I turned to Sharon and said, "So, is that a clue?"

"More than we had before, so yes, that is a clue. I think we need to head up to the pawnshop and do a little investigating on that end."

I could see the excitement in her eyes. And I also got the distinct feeling that this might take longer than just one day.

Chapter Twenty-Five

While Sharon and I were heading up to the pawnshop, Bobby and the Jamaicans were plotting how they would track down the loot. Bobby, Winston, and Fitzroy knew they had to come up with a plan since Sinclair was pissed. They just weren't sure what they should do. Sinclair and Ricketts summoned them all to the back porch of the First Colony Inn.

Sinclair said, "So, for all four of you, what is your plan for finding the treasure booty?"

Ricketts replied, "Well, sir, these three guys know their way around this area, so I think they need to start knocking on some doors to find out where the other two treasure hunters are hiding out."

"So, can you three track these two guys down? So that you know, we don't know how to find them is not an acceptable response."

Winston said, "Mr. Sinclair, we do know several people, and Bobby knows even more, but we don't know where to start. They told their parents that they were just diving for a few days, and their parents don't know where they are. We know a few people who are friends with them, and we can check with them, but if their parents don't know where they are, I doubt that any of their friends know their location. Both guys have spent a good portion of their lives here, so they know a lot of places to hide. I don't know how to track them down."

Sinclair reached into his coat pocket and pulled out a small-caliber pistol. He said, "Gentlemen, I'm very unimpressed with your plan. Do you see this gun? I think you may need to rethink your plan and show me some ways where we are likely to be successful. Think hard and think fast, gentlemen."

All three took big gulps in their throats. Bobby said, "Sir, we could go around to a couple of bars and restaurants in the area. There are some popular places where many of the locals hang out, and maybe someone has heard something. It's a place to start."

Sinclair smiled and replaced his gun in his pocket. He said to Ricketts, "See. Proper motivation can lead to accurate results. Okay, you three make the rounds of local haunts. Ricketts and I won't be much help, so we will stay here. I have some business I can conduct by phone and online, and Ricketts probably does, too. But, let me remind you three that going to the cops or trying to run will end poorly for you. Many men on my payroll will do whatever I ask them to do. If you try to run, they will find you, no matter where you run to. My men are very motivated and even more relentless. I don't care where you run to. They will find you and kill you. And it won't be just a bullet to the head, and it will be a long and painful death, so don't even think of trying to screw me on this. It will not end well for you. Oh, and I'll tell them to include your family and friends in the takedown, so if you call the cops or run, it won't be just your lives at stake, but everyone you love and care about."

Again, all three choked just a bit on the threat. Fitzroy said, "Sir, I can guarantee that we'll get a lead on where they might be. We will not disappoint you."

"That would certainly be in your best interest," said Sinclair.

Bobby, Winston, and Fitzroy got into Bobby's car. At first, the three of them said nothing because they had nothing to say. Finally, Winston said, "So where should we start?"

Bobby said, "We've been using Sam and Omie's, so I think that's a good place to start. Bartenders always overhear things, and people talk to them a lot. Maybe someone at Sam and Omie's has heard something about where Jim and Henry might be."

As they set off driving, Bobby said to the others, "Okay, guys, I don't want to get murdered by these Jamaican mobsters, but I'm also not feeling very good with myself by getting information about Jim and Henry. Those two Jamaicans will do whatever it takes to get the loot they want. Hell, they may kill us all even if they get the treasure, just to tie up any loose ends."

Winston said, "I agree. If we somehow track down Jim and Henry, Sinclair and Ricketts are certainly willing to do whatever it takes to get the booty. Maybe we should just take our chances with going to the cops. They can protect us, can't they?

"They could protect us for a while, I guess, but not forever. Plus, I don't want to look over my shoulder for the rest of my life," said Fitzroy.

Bobby said, "We don't have any easy choices here. I think, for the time being, we play along with the mobsters. If we find out something about Jim and Henry, we don't give the Jamaicans all the facts to help protect Jim and Henry. Maybe we'll get lucky, and Sinclair will get tired of looking for Jim and Henry, and he and Ricketts will just go back to Jamaica."

"That's not much of a plan," said Winston, "But I don't have a better one right now."

The three of them drove down to Sam and Omie's. The place wasn't very crowded, so they just pulled up chairs at the bar. The bartender they knew came over, and they all asked for draft beers. Once the beers arrived, the three sat at the bar and pretended to be discussing sports and fishing. They knew they couldn't just launch into asking about Jim and Henry.

After they had finished their first round, they signaled to the bartender for another round. Bobby seized the opportunity to inquire about Jim and Henry when he came back. He asked, "So how have things been going lately?"

"Business has been okay. It seems like many people extended their vacations, plus we still have folks down here doing some fishing and diving. Of course, the tragedy of Noah Spencer's apparent murder has everyone pretty shook up.

"I know. I hope the cops have some luck finding out who did it. By the way, speaking of diving, I was wondering if you've seen or heard from Jim or Henry? They were close to Noah, and I was wondering how they're handling his death."

The bartender replied, "Haven't seen them in a while. I even heard they didn't make Noah's funeral, which is really weird given how close they were. It's also funny because I just had two out-of-towners asking about Jim and Henry."

Bobby said, "What did you tell them?"

"Not much, just that they seem to have dropped off the radar. No one seems to know where they are, but I told them they might want to try your dad's pawnshop. Rumor is that they found some treasure, so maybe they went out looking for more. Still weird they didn't make Noah's funeral."

Bobby nodded and said, "Yeah, that is strange. I know Noah brought in a couple of pieces, but that's about all I know about. Maybe you're right, and they are looking for more."

The three nodded at each other, quickly finished their beers, paid their tab, and headed out the door. Winston said, "So, do we have something we can give the Jamaicans?"

Fitzroy replied, "I guess we can tell them about the two people looking for Jim and Henry. Maybe knowing someone else is looking will get them to leave."

Bobby said, "You don't believe that, and neither do I, but it's some info we can give them. Maybe buy us a little more time to figure out how we're going to get out of this nightmare."

"Nightmare is the right word," said Winston. "We've got to find a way out of this thing."

Bobby said, "Easier said than done. But we've got to give them something, so we give them the new people asking questions. I don't like getting innocents in trouble, but we don't have a lot of choices. Gotta take care of ourselves for right now."

Winston slumped his head and said, "Boy, I wish I'd never heard of sunken treasure."

Bobby said, "Don't we all."

Chapter Twenty-Six

We found the pawnshop up at Kill Devil Hills and entered. It looked like a nice place with some pretty decent items for sale. The guy who looked like the owner, the bartender said his name is Fred Biltmore, was talking to a couple looking at some old albums. It's incredible to me how vinyl has made such a comeback. People are buying old record players and stocking up on vintage albums, even ones that are scratched. I just stick with my iPhone and Spotify. I did have a few album covers that I had framed and had them hanging on my office wall and one at home in the living room. Even though I'd rather hear the music electronically, I do enjoy looking at some of the album covers from my youth. Good memories, J. Geils Band, Allman Brothers, and the Nighthawks, to name a few, but scratchy vinyl was not my thing.

After the couple looking at vinyl left, the owner came over to us. He said, "Hi, folks. Welcome to my shop. Is there anything, in particular, you're looking for? I can point you in the right direction if we have it."

I said, "Actually, we're not here looking for antiques or collectibles. We wanted to ask you a couple of questions about the kid who got killed over on the sound."

"You two cops?"

"I'm a Philadelphia police officer, but I'm not acting in any official capacity down here," said Sharon. "My friend and I were the ones who found the body, and we're just doing a little investigating as to why this might have happened. We're not going to step on the local police's toes, but since we got involved, we're just curious."

"It's just such a shame what happened. Noah had been into my shop here just a few days before he was killed."

I inquired, "We had heard about that from the bartender down at Sam and Omie's. Heard Noah brought in

107

a couple of pirate treasure items.   Can you tell us about them?"

"He brought in two pieces. I didn't know that much about them since I deal in more collectibles than antiques, but I did a little online searching and found that the pieces were likely pretty old and probably worth some pretty serious money. I told him that my appraisal was just a guess, and he needed to take them to a reputable antique appraiser to get a better idea of worth."

I asked, "Where did he say he got them?"

Fred replied, "He said he was going through some of his grandmother's stuff and just happened upon them. Said that the two items were the only things he found."

Sharon said, "So I guess it's the cop in me, but I have to ask: Did you believe him?"

"Funny you ask that. I had a weird feeling when he told me how he acquired them. I knew Noah's family were solidly middle class, but the pieces he showed me were likely worth a lot of dough. I just couldn't see how his grandmother had gotten them, but to be honest, I didn't give it that much thought. Noah wasn't asking me to sell the items for him, so their provenance was not my problem. If he had wanted me to sell them, I would have needed more information about where they came from."

"After Noah's murder, did you tell the cops about the things he brought in here?" asked Sharon.

"Actually, no, I didn't. Really didn't think that one had anything to do with the other."

Sharon frowned and said, "Sorry, I don't mean to be rude, but you didn't think Noah bringing invaluable treasure items and then getting killed might be related?"

Fred lowered his head and said, "You know what, you're right? I didn't see a connection, but now that you mention it, they probably did have something in common. I'll call the police as soon as we're finished here and let them know about the items he brought in. Damn, I'm such an idiot for not seeing it for myself."

"Don't kick yourself too much," said Sharon. "It's only been a couple of days. If the booty he brought in was somehow linked to his death, that trail has not gone cold yet. But, yes, you need to contact the local police as soon as possible. Just so you know, we were the ones who found the body in the sound, so we've spent some time with the cops describing what we saw. I can tell you that as of yesterday, they didn't have much to go on, so anything you can tell them would be helpful."

"I'll get right on it."

Sharon inquired, "Anything else you could tell us that might help?"

"Well, there is one other slightly strange thing. My son, Bobby, works in the shop with me. He texted me the other day that he was taking some time off from the shop to fish. He does that now and then, but he usually gives me more notice than this. Plus, he told me he would be very busy fishing, so he might not be in contact for a few days. Also, I'm a little surprised that he didn't go to Noah's funeral, even though I can't say they were close. My wife and I went, and we're not that close to Noah's parents at all. It just seemed like the right thing to do. Bobby is usually a better person than that. I have to say I was a little disappointed in him. But two of Noah's best friends, Jim Norman and Henry Riddick, didn't make it either. Their parents were distraught with them and worried because neither family had heard from their son in a few days. They got an email that Jim and Henry were going to do some diving and would be out of touch, which didn't worry the families at first because they do that now and then. But naturally, Noah's death got them worried about their kids, but Jim and Henry have gone dark."

"Just so you know, I've been a cop for many years, and I've learned over the years to generally not believe in coincidences. I have to say that my first reaction is that there is some link between your son and Noah's death. I don't know what it is just yet, but I think we'll stick around the Outer Banks for a few more days to check some things out."

"Do you think that Bobby might be in trouble?"

"Not sure, but I think you should contact him and find out what he's up to."

"I've tried to call and text him over the last couple of days to find out where he is and what he's up to. I only got one text back that he's fine, just doing a little fishing, but he's been really busy, so he hasn't had time to call me back. I have to admit that Bobby sometimes falls off the radar scope now and then. He just gets involved in something and forgets to give good ole dad a call."

I said, "Well, I'm not a cop, but I would leave him a voicemail and text telling him that it's important that he get in touch with you. You deserve to know that he is okay."

Fred said, "I'm going to call the police first and tell them about the treasure Noah brought in, and then I'm going to rattle my son's cage a lot that he should get in touch. Like I said; generally, he's a good kid and very responsible, so this is a little weird. It makes me worried."

Sharon said, "He's probably just your usual college-aged kid who too busy doing his own thing to call his dad. I wouldn't worry about it, but you should make sure you get him to check-in."

With that, Sharon and I shook hands with Fred and headed out the door. As we got into the car, I asked, "You don't believe that the booty and Noah's death aren't directly related, do you?"

"Of course not, but now I think we have another clue to use to track down what's going on. Sorry, Ben, but I think we're going to have to extend our stay here at OBX for a few more days."

Like I was surprised about that!

Chapter Twenty-Seven

Bobby, Winston, and Fitzroy headed back to the First Colony to check in with Sinclair and Ricketts. They knew they didn't have much to report, but they figured the longer they waited, the angrier Sinclair and Ricketts would be.

They went to Sinclair's room and knocked on the door. Sinclair opened it, and they saw that Ricketts was also in the room. Sinclair asked, "So you three have been out for a while. I hope you brought us some good news about finding the treasure."

Winston said, "Sir, we have some news, but I'm not sure it's good. We went down to a local bar, and the bartender told us two other people were asking around about Jim and Henry. Apparently, the guy is a professor, so he's not much of a problem, but the other is a female homicide cop from Philadelphia."

Sinclair slammed his hand on the table where he was sitting. "That is exactly the type of shit we don't need right now. Do these two have any information we don't have about the two other treasure hunters?"

Bobby said, "We don't think so. The bartender gave them info about Noah going to my dad's pawnshop and the treasure he brought in to be looked at. I would guess that the two new players went to my dad's store, but I doubt he knows anything about Jim's and Henry's location. I could call him and ask about it, but I don't really want to get him involved. Plus, he might go to the cops if he doesn't believe me about that I'm just out fishing. He knows the local cops very well, and it would be easy to get their attention."

Sinclair slammed his hand down again. "Son of a bitch. I don't need more people looking for those two idiots with the treasure." He turned to Ricketts and said, "I need you to take care of these two new problems."

"But, sir, do you mean that you want me to kill them?"

"No, we don't need more dead bodies. If it seems like there is a crime wave going on in this shitty little town, the local cops may call in the feds, and then we might have to just leave without the rest of the booty. I want you to scare the shit out of them so that they will just leave and never come back."

Ricketts said, "But, sir, one is a Philly cop. She's probably seen a lot in her career, so she's not going to be that easy to scare."

One more time, Sinclair slammed his hand down and said, "I'm tired of hearing excuses from everyone. I want you to get those two out of here, so we can focus on getting the treasure." He turned to Bobby and said, "Do you know where they are staying?"

"Yes, sir. They are right here at the First Colony. I sort of know one of the front desk operators. I can probably get him to tell us which room they are in."

"Then do that, and then Ricketts and I will figure out how to offer them some encouragement to leave."

Bobby took the elevator down to the first floor and went to the front desk. The guy he knew was reluctant to tell him anything about our room, but finally, he gave Bobby our location.

When Bobby returned to Sinclair's room, he said, "I found out which room they are in. But there are other people on both sides of their room, so whatever you're going to do, you probably need to be quiet."

Ricketts said, "How the fuck am I supposed to scare the shit out of them and be quiet about it?"

Bobby hesitated at first but then said, "The guy at the front desk said they usually take a walk on the beach after dinner."

Ricketts smiled and said, "Then that is my opportunity. Can the front desk guy give you a heads-up if they are headed out for a walk?"

"I suppose he could," said Bobby, "But I don't know why he would want to do that. He could get in a lot of trouble here at the hotel."

Sinclair reached into his pocket and took out a wad of cash. He peeled one hundred dollars off in twenties and said to Bobby, "Hand this to him and say that you want a text message when they are headed out. After you get it, you text Ricketts, and he'll take it from there."

Bobby slowly took the money. He then said to Sinclair, "But, sir, I'm still not sure he'll want to do it. Plus, what do I tell him about why I want to know when they are leaving?"

Sinclair moved his face close to Bobby's and said, "I don't give a fuck what you tell him about why. I just want you to make it happen so Ricketts here can have a talk with them out on the beach."

Bobby's hands were shaking, but he tried not to let Sinclair and Ricketts see it. He had no idea if he could get the front desk guy to go along with this crazy idea, but he knew he needed to try. Actually, he needed to succeed because it looked like Sinclair was losing patience, and Bobby figured that was a bad thing for him and his two Jamaican partners

Bobby said to Sinclair, "Sir, maybe a better thing to do is that I find a spot to hang out down by the front desk and have the guy just give me the heads up when he sees the two we're looking for heading to the beach. That way, I can tell Mr. Ricketts what they look like."

"Do whatever you need to; just make sure that Ricketts gets a chance to have a chat with them."

Bobby left Sinclair's room and headed down to the front desk, and went up to see the front desk guy. He told the guy what he wanted to say to him when he saw the professor and the cop. Naturally, the front desk guy asked why. Bobby said to him that he had been thinking about a job in law enforcement, and he wanted to talk to the Philly cop. The guy gave him a strange look until Bobby offered him the C note to tell him when they were headed out. Struck the front desk guy as weird, but a hundred dollars was nice to have in his pocket. Bobby found a seat near the main entrance and parked there, waiting for his big moment with the deal in place.

While all this was happening, Sharon and I were at The Jolly Roger again, having scallops and oysters. We enjoyed the meal immensely, and then we headed back to the First Colony.

We went back to our room and sat for a few minutes, and then we headed out for our nightly walk. We didn't know we had a shadow watching us in the lobby, but Bobby did his job and contacted Ricketts to let him know it was showtime if he wanted to talk to us.

We got to the beach and found that it was empty. We had the whole place to ourselves. We started walking over close to the ocean so we could hear it. We were holding hands which is not something we do that much, but the sea is very romantic for both of us.

Sharon noticed someone else coming down to the beach as we were walking. A single guy. We didn't think anything of it until the guy caught up to us and said, "Could I have a moment of your time?"

I turned and said, "Sure, what's on your mind?"

"I would like to encourage you to discontinue your search for the guys who might have more of the pirate treasure."

Sharon shouted, "Who the fuck do you think you are?"

"I'm the guy who has a gun in his coat pocket. Does that clarify who I am?"

"Yeah, it does. You're the second person on this beach who is carrying a gun." With that, Sharon pulled her service revolver out of her jacket and pointed at him. "Does this clarify who I am?"

Ricketts was shocked at first and didn't know what to do. However, mob instinct took over, and he pulled his gun from his coat pocket. As he started to raise the gun at us, Sharon shot him in the arm, holding the gun. The guy screamed, the gun fell to the ground, and he took off running.

I turned to Sharon and said, "Nice shot, but what the hell are you doing carrying your weapon when we're out for a walk on the beach at the Outer Banks?"

Sharon replied, "Don't know, but somehow I had a weird feeling about how this whole event has been going down. A lot of intrigue and possibly even some carnage, so I just decided to err on the side of caution and brought my piece."

"Glad you did, but someday we're going to have to discuss how you get these feelings. Creeps me out a bit."

"Just think of me as adding spice to your life."

Chapter Twenty-Eight

We told the front desk manager about the incident as soon as we got back to our hotel, and then we dialed 911. I gave the operator a brief rundown of what happened and that we were fine and didn't need medical assistance. Our two favorite Outer Banks cops, Officers Brown and Jones, were at the hotel less than ten minutes later.

Sharon asked, "Don't you guys ever sleep?"

Jones replied, "We do, but it was just luck that we were on call tonight. It has been tranquil all evening, so we just came right over when we got the 911 call. Normally, it would be the emergency personnel, but we took the call since we were available, and you said you didn't need medical assistance. The operator told us what happened, but naturally, we'd like to hear the full story from you."

"Want me to do it again, Ben?"

"Since you're the one packing a gun, I think you would do the best job of explaining what transpired."

Sharon smiled, "Well, to be honest, it's a pretty short story to tell. Ben and I went to dinner at the Jolly Roger. We came home about 8 p.m., sat for a few minutes in our room, and then decided to take a walk on the beach. Not much moon out, so it was pretty dark, but we could hear the waves. At first, we thought we had the beach to ourselves, but then a guy with a thick accent came up close from behind us. He didn't say that much except that we would do well to leave the Outer Banks and do it quickly. I didn't take well to his suggestion and told him to do so. Then he reached into his pocket to show us the outline of the gun he had. I'm sure he figured we would just run for the hills back to our hotel, pack up, and leave right then. It didn't go that way. I had my service revolver with me, and I took it out to show the guy. I'm sure he was shocked, and he reached for his gun in his pocket. As he got the gun out and started to point it at us, I put a round into his right arm where he was holding his piece. As I said, not much moonlight, so I'm not completely sure where I got him, but I think it was in his bicep. Might have just been a flesh wound. Hard to tell in the dark. He screamed, dropped his gun, and took off running. I decided not to pursue him because I didn't know if he had any associates around who might take exception to him being shot. Ben had a cloth in his jacket, and we used that to pick up the guy's gun, naturally trying not to disturb any possible fingerprints. I have the gun covered with the cloth in a bag we got from the front desk. It's right here." With that, Sharon handed Brown the bag.

Brown took the bag, opened it just to see the contents, and then closed it. He said to Sharon, "Did you recognize the guy at all?"

She said, "As I said, it was pretty dark, so hard to see. But I didn't recognize him or the accent. Anything Ben?"

"Same as you. Nothing that I could put my finger on."

Jones asked, "What about the accent? Any ideas?"

I said, "Sounded like it was from the islands. Maybe Jamaica, although the only Jamaican accent I'm sure of is Bob Marley. But it was pretty thick."

Sharon continued, "I'd guess Jamaican, too. We have a small contingent of Jamaican mobsters in the Philly area, so I've heard some Jamaican accents, and this fella sounded pretty close to one."

Brown asked, "I'm guessing you didn't get a good enough look at him that you could pick him out of a lineup or mug shot book."

Sharon replied, "Maybe, but I couldn't be sure."

Jones inquired about Sharon's shot. "So, you think you hit him in the right arm. Any idea if you grazed him or if you hit him dead on?"

"I think I grazed him in the bicep. He moved just as I fired otherwise. I would have put one right in his arm. He might still need to seek some sort of medical treatment and probably soon. I don't think it's a wound that you could just wrap with a towel and be okay. There can't be that many places in this area where he could get that sort of treatment, is there?"

Brown said, "We've got the urgent care facility you know about and the Outer Banks hospital. Urgent care isn't open right now, and we've put the hospital on alert about anyone with a gunshot wound coming in. They'll let us know if the guy comes in, but I told them not to deny him treatment because if he's packing a piece, he could hurt someone if they say no treatment. The guy is probably quite desperate right now. I'm sure you rocked him some, Sharon, by having your gun with you. He figured he could just scare you off, and that would be it. Didn't plan on having to return fire."

"I've learned from too many years as a Philly cop that you can never assume anything. In Philly, making assumptions about your adversary can get you killed. Guy's lucky I didn't decide just to go center mass and put him down."

Brown asked, "Speaking of that; I know you're taught to go center mass if a gun is pointed at you. Why didn't you put the guy down?"

"That's an excellent question. And I hate to admit it, but I was going center mass. I wasn't going to screw around, but the guy dove to the side just as I fired. I should have put another one in him, but he turned and fled very quickly. As I said, I decided not to pursue him if he had partners nearby. I doubted he did because he would have brought them with him, but I determined it wasn't a good plan to chase him. He was wounded, and I had his gun, but he could have been carrying another, so I decided to let you guys track him down. I figured the Outer Banks is an isolated place, so I decided not to pursue him."

Brown smiled and said, "And somewhere during all this excitement, you remembered that you have no authority down here, and you are not supposed to be chasing people with a gun in your hand."

"That did cross my mind after the guy took off running. I figured you guys would likely consider the first shot self-defense, but if I chased after him, I might be exceeding my limited authority down here."

Jones also smiled and said, "Yeah, that might have gotten you in a bit of trouble with the district attorney down here. Protecting Ben and yourself is one thing. Running after the guy is another.

Sharon laughed a little and said, "Figured that. Anyway, that's about all I can think of to add to the events of the evening. Ben, you got anything you want to add?" I shook my head. "So, I'm guessing this is where you tell Ben and me that we need to leave the Outer Banks immediately and that local authorities will take it from here?"

"That's right," said Brown, "But you're not going to do that, are you?"

"Absolutely. I'm going upstairs to pack as soon as you two leave. Overall, I think Ben and I have had a great time down here, but it's time to head home."

Jones said, "I don't believe you."

Neither did I!

Chapter Twenty-Nine

Ricketts took his car and looked for a place to hide. Once he had found a deserted house and had a garage where he could hole up, he called Sinclair. He told him that he had been shot but that it was only a grazing hit and that he thought that just covering it with a towel he had found outside the house where he was would do for now. However, Ricketts said that he couldn't return to the First Colony because the cop who had shot him was staying there, and he was sure she had informed the police. Sinclair told Ricketts to head down to Jeanette's Pier and remain in his car until Sinclair got there.

Sinclair got his driver to take the limo down to Jeanette's Pier. It only took about twenty minutes. Ricketts saw him coming and flashed his lights. It was late and dark, so Ricketts wasn't worried about anyone seeing them.

Sinclair had his limo pulled to the side of Ricketts' car. He motioned for Ricketts to get into the limo. Sinclair didn't seem particularly interested in Ricketts' injury. He just yelled and said, "What the fuck happened?"

"Sir, the woman cop had a gun in her jacket pocket. I didn't know it was there, and she had it out before I could get mine out."

"You stupid shit! Why didn't you have your gun already out?"

"We planned to frighten them off and not to shoot anyone. I thought I could do that with a dire warning."

Sinclair snorted, "Yeah, well, you weren't successful with that plan, were you? Even though I am royally pissed right now, I guess I should ask about your injury?"

"She only grazed me, Sir. I was bleeding some, but I wrapped a towel I found around my arm, and most of the bleeding has stopped. I'm lucky that I dove right before she fired otherwise, or she would have done much more damage."

"Do you need medical assistance?"

"I don't think so. I doubt there is an all-night pharmacy down here, but I think I'll need some antibiotics and a gauze wrap once one opens. We can't take a chance going to the hospital or even urgent care. I'm sure the cop has contacted the local police, and they have put out a BOLO for someone with an injured arm. I think if I get some medicine, I'll be okay for the time being. If I start to have pain or other symptoms, I will let you know."

"Ricketts, you should know by now that I don't give a shit about whether you are in pain or not. I just want to get the treasure and get out of here. If you need medical attention, the quicker we find what we want, the quicker we can get out of here and back to Jamaica. I have doctors and nurses on call back there."

"Then what is our next step, Sir?"

"I've already contacted one of my best men down in Jamaica, Delroy Williams, and he is flying out to Norfolk first thing tomorrow. When he gets here, we will up the stakes and force these young idiots to give up the treasure. We will take someone they know, maybe a family member, and hold them hostage if we have to. I decided that if that was a possibility, then we might need a little more firepower."

"I know Delroy, but we have never worked together. I've heard he is exceptional with a gun."

"He is one of my best shots," said Sinclair. "He should be here by early afternoon. Once he arrives, we'll huddle and figure out the next steps, but we will be moving quickly."

"Sir, where should I go until he arrives? I can't take a chance and go back to the First Colony, can I?"

"No, you clearly can't, and I can't stay there long. I'm having my driver take me back to collect my things. I'll get yours, too. Here is $500. Go find us a couple of hotel rooms away from the First Colony. Once you do, call me with the location. We'll try to get a little sleep before Delroy gets here.

And I'm not heartless. We'll try to find you some medication once the stores open. We can't take you to a medical facility as you rightfully said. The cops surely have notices posted, and the cops would be on us in minutes."

"Don't worry, Mr. Sinclair. I can handle a little pain. I do want some antibiotics, so I don't get an infection, but other than that, I'll be okay."

For the first time, Sinclair finally showed just an ounce of compassion. He said, "Don't worry, Ricketts. I'm going to make sure that you are well compensated for your efforts once we get the loot."

"Thank you, sir. I'm sure you will be generous."

"That is, of course, unless we are unsuccessful in getting the treasure. If that happens, you may end up dead."

Ricketts gasped for some air, but he wasn't surprised by the comment. Such was the life, or death, of a Jamaican mobster.

Chapter Thirty

We got up early even though we were out very late with Jones and Brown. I knew that Sharon was now hooked on solving this whole thing. In particular, she wants to find the guy who jumped us on the beach and whether he has a partner or boss.

I said, "So, I know you're not going to let this go, so how do you want to play it?"

"I'm not sure I have a good idea on how to proceed. It's clear that Noah's death is related to the guy who jumped us, and I'm guessing the treasure Noah brought into the pawnshop is what's driving all the Jamaican, or whatever island, interest in this area. But I don't think we have any good leads right now. You got any ideas?"

"Well, Fred told us that two of Noah's best friends, Jim and Henry, have fallen off the radar. Maybe we should contact their parents and see if they know anything about the jewelry Noah brought into the pawnshop. It's not a great idea, but it is one."

"And how are we going to find out about his friends' families?"

"You're going to use your considerable feminine charms and get our new pals, Officers Brown and Jones, to give us someone to talk to."

"You do know that they would like it much more if we just left the Outer Banks and went back to Philly."

"Of course, but they might be willing to help a fellow law enforcement professional do a little bit of digging. I'm not suggesting that you offer to solve the crime for them, just to do a little legwork. They might even appreciate the assistance."

Sharon chuckled and said, "Okay, you have done enough of this detecting stuff to know that cops don't usually want any help, and it's even less likely they're going to want help from two non-locals."

"Worth a shot unless you've got a better idea. Do you?"

"No, and you know that. Fine, I'll give them a call and see if they can just get us a name and address for one of the families."

Sharon went into the bedroom of our hotel room to have a little privacy. I just turned on the TV to catch up on the news. There are times I'm not sure watching the news does anything but depress me, but I sometimes just can't help myself. Maybe I should switch to one of the ridiculous daytime game shows. Find out if The Price is Really Right.

After a few minutes, Sharon came out with a bit of a smile on her face. She said, "I guess I'm just not used to cops in small towns. Brown was more than happy to give me the name and address of Jim's and Henry's parents. He wished me luck after I promised to keep him informed if we found anything interesting. Never would happen in Philly, but gotta love that Southern hospitality."

"Then pick one, we'll see if they're home, and if so, we'll grab some coffee and donuts and make a trip. You never know; we've lucked out on things like this more than once."

Sharon decided to call the Norman family and the mother of the house, May, was at home. At first, she was reluctant to talk to Sharon, but Sharon convinced her that we were just trying to help find her son and make sure he was okay. After a bit more hesitation, May gave us her address and said she would be home for the next couple of hours.

We got the coffee and donuts and plowed through them on the way to the Norman home. The Normans lived on the sound side of Nags Head down by Kitty Hawk Kites. We quickly found their home, and we knocked on the door.

A woman who looked to be in her fifties opened the door. I asked, "Ms. Norman. My name is Ben Stone, and this is Sharon Levin. Sharon called about discussing your son and his friend, Henry."

"Yes, please come in." She took us to the living room. She then asked, "Can I get you something to drink?"

Sharon said, "No, we're fine. First off, I need to tell you why we ask about Jim and Henry. Ben and I were out doing some sailing, and we were the ones who found Noah's body. Naturally, we notified the local police. Then last night, Ben and I were walking on the beach over by the First Colony, and a gentleman came up to us and threatened us that we needed to leave the Outer Banks. I could tell the guy was armed, but so was I. I got my gun out more quickly and shot him. I think I only grazed him, but it was hard to tell in the dark. Anyway, with all this intrigue going on, Ben and I decided to do some detective work ourselves, and one thing we thought of was finding out about Noah's friends, and your son, Jim, is one of his closest. Anyway, that's why we are here."

"I'm thrilled you came. My husband and I have been very worried about Jim since the incident with Noah. Noah, Jim, and Henry have been best friends since grade school. The fact that Jim and Henry didn't come to Noah's funeral tells my husband and me that something is wrong. We've contacted the police, and they put out an all-points bulletin, but nothing has been found yet. Jim sent us an email a few days ago saying that he and Henry were diving and wouldn't be in touch for a few days. To be honest, my husband and I didn't think much of it until what happened to Noah. We've tried emailing, texting, calling, and still nothing. My husband has gotten a few friends together, and they are out looking for Jim and probably Henry, but so far, no luck. I know it in my bones that something bad has happened. This is very unlike Jim."

Sharon inquired, "Well, certainly your husband would have some good ideas of where to look. Anything you can share where we might look, too?"

"My husband started, of course, with their apartments, but nothing. We tried some of their usual haunts for food and beverage, but nothing. My husband and his buddies are now starting to work their way down Hatteras Island. Many little towns have all sorts of places to hide if that's what they are doing. But there are a lot of them, so my husband called me just about an hour ago and said they hadn't had any luck yet. But he's going to keep trying."

I asked, "Where are they now, if I can ask?"

"They have made their way to Avon, one of the upper locales of the island."

Sharon asked, "Ms. Norman, I know this might be a long shot, but if you had to guess, where do you think Jim and maybe Henry might be?"

"They love Hatteras because it has a few more places where they can head out to dive. Of course, my husband knows that, and he's heading that way, but he's just working his way through the small towns on the way to Hatteras."

"Well, thank you so much for your help. Ben and I may just add to the number of people looking for Jim, but we'll likely give it a try. Can we get your husband's cell phone number in case we find something down his way?"

"Of course." She gave Sharon her husband's cell phone. "And thank you for helping. I guess the more people hunting for them, the more likely they'll be found."

Sharon said, "We'll help in any way that we can." With that, we said goodbye.

As we got into our car, I asked, "So, do you have a plan laid out in your mind yet?"

"Well, I think we're going to head down to Hatteras, but I'm going to try to call in some reinforcements."

"Reinforcements? From Philly?"

"Nope. I'm going to check in with our new buddies with the FBI. They have some experience finding people, but more importantly, they can get us some info on the guy from the beach. They've got databases on everyone and everything. Much more than they have here in the Outer Banks and probably a lot more than even Philly."

I smiled and said, "I like it. Now we're bringing in the big guns."

Chapter Thirty-One

While Sharon and I were figuring out our way down to Hatteras Island, Bobby and all of his new Jamaican friends were waiting at the new hotel for Delroy Williams to arrive. At around 1 p.m., there was a knock at the hotel room door. Sinclair answered it, said hello to the person at the door, and opened it so that the new player could enter.

Bobby was shocked when he saw the new guy, Delroy Williams. He was at least 6'6" tall with muscles bulging in every direction. He had tattoos all over his arms. Bobby could only assume that he had similar tattoos all over his body. His head was shaved, but even though it wasn't warm outside, Williams' head was still glistening in the sun. In short, Bobby knew at once that this was a scary guy.

Sinclair said, "As all of you know, this is Delroy Williams. Williams, I know you already know Ricketts. These three, you can call them Larry, Curly, and Moe for all I care, are the ones who know their way around this shitty little area. They're going to help us find the treasure, and then we're going to get the fuck out of here. I've already had a motivational discussion with them, and I'm confident they're going to be successful in our venture. Towards that end, where do you three think we should head out to right now?"

Bobby decided it might be best if he spoke for the three. "Sir, if I had to guess, I would think that they have gone down farther on Hatteras Island. There are a lot of places to hide down toward the end of Hatteras Island. Many little towns have many empty rental houses available because this is off-season."

"We don't have time to go through a bunch of shitty little towns," replied Sinclair. "I want to know where is the most likely place they would hide?"

"Sir, if you're making me take a guess, I would say that they would be down towards the end of the island. Hatteras

133

Village has more homes, and you could quickly get over to Ocracoke if you need to. From there, you can take another ferry to the mainland."

Sinclair cracked an evil-looking smile and said, "Well, the well-being of you and your two buddies depends on making the right decision on where the other two might be, so if you think Hatteras is the place, then that is where we will go."

Bobby shook just a bit and said, "But, sir, I can't guarantee that Hatteras will be the place. They may have already left the Outer Banks. For all, I know they are hiding in another state. Maybe even a different country like Canada. I'm trying to help, but it's still a guess."

Sinclair said, "Well, for the health of you three, be right. I don't care at all what it takes, but I have spent enough time here, Ricketts got shot, and I still don't have the other treasure. So, whatever it takes, you better be right."

Bobby looked at Winston and Fitzroy. All three were scared beyond belief, but they knew they were essentially trapped. Finally, Winston decided to add, "Mr. Sinclair, Fitzroy, and I agree with Bobby that Hatteras Village is our best bet. We should get started down there. The two people Mr. Ricketts had an altercation with might also still be hunting for Jim and Henry. We need to get ahead of them."

Sinclair said, "That's the attitude I'm looking for. I'll take Delroy in my limo while Ricketts takes you three with him in his car. And just a reminder, when we get down to this Hatteras Village, don't even think of trying to wander off. Mr. Williams here has a pretty bad temper, and you don't want him annoyed with you."

Bobby gulped and said, "No, sir. We are committed to helping you find the treasure."

While this action was happening with the Jamaican contingent, Sharon was getting ready to call either Emily Keen or Randall Jones of the FBI. She decided on trying Emily first.

Surprisingly, Keen picked up right away. She just said, "Keen."

Sharon responded, "Emily, it's Sharon Levin from the down at the Outer Banks. How are you doing?"

"Sharon, nice to hear from you. I'm doing okay. Been busy with some drug trafficking up in Boston, but I haven't had to travel that much. How are you and Ben doing? You're back in Philly by now, right?"

"We're fine, but we are still down at the Outer Banks. We stayed a couple of extra days, but then we got involved in a murder down here. Ben and I were sailing out in the sound, and we found a body that had washed ashore. We called the local authorities, gave them all the info we had, and didn't think any more of it. Then the next night, we went for a walk on the beach, and a Jamaican guy tried to run us out of here. He reached for a gun, but I happened to have my gun with me, and I got mine out first and winged him on the arm. Because of that, we started doing a little digging, and it seems there might be some pirate treasure down here that these Jamaicans are willing to kill for. My cop instinct will not let me just walk away from it, so we're still down here doing some sleuthing."

"Damn, leave it to you two to not just have a nice little work slash vacation trip. It seems like crazy stuff follows you two. Anyway, what can I do for you?"

"We were just wondering if you have any information about the Jamaican mob. I'm guessing, but the guy who tried to scare us off the other night carried himself like a made guy. We have a bit of the Jamaican mob in Philly, but I figured you had access to much more information. I thought maybe you could get us a list of some big-time Jamaican mobsters, maybe with pictures, and we could get a handle on who these guys might be. Any info would be helpful."

"Sure, Sharon. Happy to help. I've got a couple of things with the Boston case that I need to take care of first, but then I'll pull what we have on the Jamaican mob. I know we've been tracking them for a long time, so I can probably get you some relevant info. But, and you probably already know this, the Jamaican mob is pretty ruthless. If you and Ben are doing a deep dive into these people, you need to be very careful."

"That's why I'm not going anywhere without my weapon. And any information you could get us would be great."

Emily said, "If I come up with anything useful, I'll give you a call."

"That's great. Thanks so much for all your help." With that, Sharon hung up. She said to Ben, "So Emily is going to help us figure out these guys might be. It's a start."

I said, "Sounds like a start. What do you want to do next?"

"Let's take May's advice and head down to Hatteras Village. We'll just wander around the village for a while and see what we see."

"Yep, I guess that right now, we're just hoping for some luck to come our way. Anyway, I suppose it's time to gas up and take a ride. At least we'll get to see some more of the sights for the Outer Banks."

"That's us. Trying to solve a murder and do so while working in some sightseeing. That is truly the definition of multitasking."

Chapter Thirty-Two

Sharon and I headed down to Hatteras Village. Along the way, we saw some of the little seaside towns: Rodanthe, Salvo, Avon, Buxton, and Frisco. They all looked very quaint with just a smattering of new buildings that seemed to focus on T-shirts and souvenirs. We also saw some restaurants that looked like they had been there a while. I noted that if we ever returned to OBX, we needed to venture down here to get even more of the local flavor.

After about an hour on the beach road, we made it into Hatteras. Since we had pictures of Jim and Henry, Sharon suggested starting our search at a local market. We found a supermarket called Food Lion and a donut shop called Duck Donuts. We decided to try the supermarket first.

We went into the Food Lion and found our way to customer service. The young lady behind the counter looked to still be in high school. She asked, "Hi, how can I help you?"

Sharon replied, "We're looking for two guys who might be down here, and we were wondering if you could help? I have pictures of them.

"Sure, no problem." She took a look at Jim and Henry and said, "I don't recognize them, but why don't I get the manager. He's in today, and he is in the store a lot more than I am."

Sharon said, "That would be great. Thanks for the help."

The customer service girl picked up her phone and paged the manager. After a few minutes, a guy who looked maybe 30 came over to where we were. "Hi, I'm Bill, and I'm the manager here. I heard you're looking for someone and that I might help."

"Yes, we're looking for two young men who do a lot of diving," replied Sharon. "Here are their pictures."

Accounting for Pirates

The guy took a look at the pictures and said, "Sure, this is Jim Norman and Henry Riddick. I was ahead of them in school, but we knew each other from playing local sports together. Not that many athletes down here on OBX, so we have to expand who can play."

"Have you seen them recently?"

"Funny you should ask. I managed one of the checkout lines the other day because a couple of folks called in sick, and I saw Jim and Henry checking out in another line. I waved and tried to say hello to them, but they seemed to be in a hurry, and we didn't connect."

Sharon asked, "Any chance you saw which way they went?"

"No. As I said, I was working, and they were in a hurry. By the way, why are you looking for them? Are they in some sort of trouble?"

"Not at all. It's just that their parents haven't heard from them in a while. We met with Jim's mom, May, and we said we'd take a look around and see if they turn up."

"Well, I've only seen them the one time. Actually, it was a bit strange because I know Jim and Henry do some diving down here, but it looked like they had packed in a lot of groceries. It looked like they were staying for a while. Seemed a little weird, but I didn't think much of it at the time."

I inquired, "Got any ideas where they might be?"

"Nah, lots of places they could rent since it's off-season. I have no idea where they landed. They might not even be in Hatteras Village. Not that many places to shop in the little towns on Hatteras Island, so people from Frisco and the like come down here."

Sharon said, "Okay, thanks a lot for the info. Maybe we'll get lucky, and they'll just show up."

Bill said, "Sorry to hear their families are worried about them. Good luck finding them."

As Sharon and I left the store, we didn't know that Bill had contacted Jim and Henry. Jim and Henry had asked that if Bill heard about anyone asking about them, he would let them know. Jim had bought a burner phone on their way down to Hatteras and left the number with Bill.

Bill called the number, and Jim immediately answered, "Bill, what's up?"

"Two people, a man, and a woman, just came in looking for you two."

"Oh shit. What did you tell them?"

"I told them you had been in to get some groceries. They said your families are worried about you. What the hell is going on?"

"Just got a little family drama. Nothing to worry about. Thanks for giving us the heads up about the people looking for us. We appreciate it." With that, Jim hung up.

Henry asked, "So what's going on? Why did Bill call?"

"Two people came into the Food Lion asking questions about us. They said they had been in contact with my mother, and that's she worried about me, but who knows if we can believe that."

"So, what do you want to do?"

"I think it's time to pack up our clothes and some of the food and head over to Ocracoke. From there, we can take the ferry to Cedar Island and get to the mainland. I think we may have to make a run for it."

"And not tell our parents?" said Henry.

"We'll tell them once we get to the mainland. In fact, once we get to Cedar Island, we can call them and tell them what's going on. And then we head inland somewhere."

"How long are we going to live like this?"

Jim said, "I don't know since I'm making this up as I'm going along, but we'll figure something out. But right now, I think we need to put some more distance between us and anyone looking for us."

"It's not a great plan, but I guess it's a plan. Let's pack up and hit the road. I guess actually hit the ferries."

While Jim and Henry were plotting their escape down to Ocracoke and then to the mainland, Bobby, Winston, and Fitzroy were having no luck tracking down Jim and Henry. Bobby knew many people up and down Hatteras Island, but no one said they had seen Jim and Henry around. While he had hoped he could at least give Sinclair something, he didn't have much to report.

In fact, just as he was hanging his head that he didn't have any news, Sinclair called. "So, what do you have to report?"

"I'm sorry, sir, but we haven't had any luck getting a lead on where they might be. I've checked in with the people I know in the area, but nothing so far."

"Needless to say, that's disappointing. However, I've had enough of this mindless searching up and down this crappy little island. You know where one or both of these guys' families live, don't you?"

Thinking quickly, Bobby said, "No, sir. I don't know where their families live. We're haven't been close for a long time, and we weren't even that close back when we were in school."

Sinclair snickered over the phone and said, "I don't believe you. I'll give you credit for trying to protect these guys, but I'm willing to bet that you know where at least one family lives. And you need to come back up here and point us in the right direction. Otherwise, I'll have Ricketts and Williams track you down, which will not be a pleasant situation for you and your new Jamaican pals. We know where your father's pawnshop is, and we'll visit him if need be. Do you get the message?"

As much as Bobby wanted to do the right thing and not give up Jim and Henry, he couldn't bring himself to put his dad in danger. He said, "Yes, I understand. And yes, I do know where Jim's parents live or at least where they used to live."

"Then the three of you should get your asses back up here, and then we're going to visit those parents. Also, trust me, if those two idiots come clean with the treasure, then I'll leave them and their families alone."

Bobby didn't believe him for a second!

Chapter Thirty-Three

Bobby, Winston, and Fitzroy reluctantly returned to the hotel where Sinclair and the other mobsters were staying. Bobby knocked on the door, and Ricketts opened it. "Come on in," he said. "Mr. Sinclair is anxious to get this started."

The three OBX guys entered the room and found Sinclair and Williams drinking coffee and watching TV. Williams shut off the TV while Sinclair said, "So where does one of the families of the two annoying little treasure hunters live?"

One last time Bobby hesitated. "As I told you, sir, it's been a long time, and I can't be sure they still live in the same house."

Sinclair jumped up and grabbed Bobby by his collar. "Stop stalling. Give us the location right now, or I'm going to have Mr. Williams explain to you the consequences of delaying."

Bobby gulped again, something he had been doing a lot of since this treasure hunting started, and said, "They used to live over on the sound side near Kitty Hawk Kites. I honestly do not remember the address, I swear."

Sinclair said, "Fine. Then Williams will ride with you three over to the house, and we'll follow in the limo. As always, don't try anything cute, or you will get hurt."

Everyone piled into the appropriate vehicle, and they headed out. Bobby decided there was no way to try to stall them anymore, so he took them directly to Jim's family's home. Both vehicles pulled into the driveway. Sinclair had Williams go up to the front door with Bobby.

Bobby knocked, and after a moment, the door opened. Jim's mom, May, stood at the doorway and immediately recognized Bobby. She said, "Bobby Biltmore. I recognized you immediately. What brings you over here?"

Williams pushed his way into the house and said, "My partners and I need a bit of your time. Why don't we go have a seat in your living room and talk?" With that, he grabbed May's arm and waved for Sinclair and the rest to come in.

Naturally, May was now scared and wanted to scream, but Williams suggested it would be beneficial if she stayed silent.

Everyone huddled in the living room, and Sinclair did the talking. "So, we need to talk to your son. Do you know how to reach him?"

"No. My son has not been in contact with us for a few days. He said that he and a friend were doing some diving. My husband and I have been worried, and my husband is down on Hatteras Island looking for him."

"So, you don't have a way to contact him?"

"We've called and left several messages, including phone calls, texts, and emails, but we've heard nothing. He sent us one email, and that's been it for almost a week ago. As I said, we've been worried, so my husband has been searching for him for two days."

Sinclair said, "Give me your cell phone and your son's number. I think I have a message that he might respond to."

May handed him her phone, and Jim's number was on her contacts. Sinclair pressed send on Jim's number, and it went straight to voicemail. Sinclair said, "Jim, I hope you listen to this voicemail. I'm also going to text and email you. My name is Lloyd Sinclair, and I am from Jamaica. I know that you and your buddy are hiding because you have some pirate treasure you want to keep. I want that treasure, and I want it soon. My associates and I are holding your mother captive in your family's home. If I don't hear back from you within two days, your mother will have a most unfortunate accident. Do not contact the police since we are holding your mother hostage, and we will use her as leverage if the cops get involved. If you and your buddy will just give up your shares of the booty, my associates and I will be on our way back to Jamaica. However much you think the treasure is worth, it's not worth your mother's life. Make the smart choice and give me what I want. And remember that the deadline for making this happen is just two days. Call or text me on your mother's phone. Again, make the smart move."

Sinclair turned to everyone and said, "Now we wait." He turned to May and said, "But for your sake, not too long, I hope."

While Sinclair was busy kidnapping and threatening Jim's mother, Sharon and I were still looking around Hatteras Village. We weren't having any more luck than Bobby and his team until we got down to where the ferry to Ocracoke was launched. We were driving through the small town just when we saw a car in line to take the ferry suddenly get out of line. I didn't have a good look at the driver, but the passenger resembled the kid named Henry we were looking for.

Once they were out of line, they pulled over to the side and stopped. I told Sharon to pull up beside them because I thought they might be the two we were looking for. She did. I got out of our car and then went to the other one. I knocked on the window, and the driver slowly rolled down his side.

I asked, "Hi, are you Jim Norman?"

He replied, "Yes, I am, but who wants to know?"

"My name is Ben Stone, and my friend over there is Sharon Levin. We've been looking for you because we were the ones who found Noah dead, and we thought you might be in danger, too."

"Noah is dead?"

"Yes, I'm sorry to say he is. You didn't know?"

Jim responded, "No, we didn't know. We've been in hiding for the last few days. Noah contacted us that a Jamaican guy threatened him if he didn't give up the pirate treasure he had. Noah recommended that we go into hiding, so we hid in a small house over on the sound. We just found out that some people were looking for us, so we were headed out to Ocracoke and then over to the mainland."

I asked, "Those two people looking for you were probably us. We think that the guy who killed Noah was part of a group where one of the guys threatened us out on the beach. The guy pulled a gun on us, but Sharon is a Philadelphia homicide cop, and she had her weapon with her. She shot the guy, probably only winged him, but we have been trying to find out what's happened since then. We've let the local police know about our involvement, and they've supported our efforts.
But my main question is: Why did you suddenly jump out of line for the ferry to Ocracoke?"

"I just got a text from some guy named Lloyd Sinclair who said that he is holding my mother captive, and if Henry and I don't give him the pirate treasure we have, he's going to harm her."

"And you just found out about this?"

"Yes, I know that my parents have been looking for me, as have Henry's parents been looking for him, but we haven't been in direct contact for a while. We lied to our parents that we were diving, and we know they have been looking for us, but we were afraid that if we made contact with our parents, it would only worry them more. We were going to make direct contact with them once we got to a safe place on the mainland."

Sharon and Henry got out of their respective cars as we spoke, and the four of us stood in the parking lot. Everyone introduced themselves, and I brought Sharon up to speed with where we were. She said, "So you two should call the police up in Nags Head and get them involved."

Jim said, "The Sinclair guy said that if we got the police involved, my mother would be harmed. I can't take that chance, can I?"

Sharon said, "Okay, I will admit that these Jamaican guys seem pretty ruthless, but you've got to do something."

I suggested, "Well. Sharon, how about you and I be the intermediaries between these two guys and the Jamaicans. The Jamaicans already know that you are armed. Maybe we can set up a meet using you to provide safety for Jim, Henry, and me, and then the guys can give up the treasure they have. By the way, I assume you're willing to give up the treasure you have."

Henry said, "Of course, it's Jim's mom. But since you two seem to be straight-shooters, I'll tell you that we have a lot more treasure hidden at Jim's family's house. We had split a relatively small amount between the three of us, and Jim and I still have our small shares. Happy to give those up to the Jamaicans."

Sharon inquired, "And Jim's mother doesn't know anything about the treasure you hid at her house?"

"No way," said Jim. "It's hidden in small hidey-hole that no one even remembers is there. We used to hide things there when we were young, but no one has even thought about it for years, at least until we decided to hide the bulk of our booty there."

Sharon said, "Well, I guess it's nice that you have a safety net, but Ben and I don't care about that very much. What we do want to do is capture the guy who threatened us and anyone else from his crew we can bring in."

Henry asked, "Would you be willing to help us set up a drop with these Jamaicans to get them the booty that they know of? They say they will leave us all alone as long as they get the treasure."

Sharon said, "I wouldn't believe them on that, but I think that Ben and I can offer some backup on that score. We can help you make the exchange with the Jamaicans, and then we immediately call the local police to get everyone some protection. There's naturally some risk with dealing with these mobsters, but I think we can minimize that risk since I am armed. Once we make the exchange and call the local police, Ben and I can help them bring one or more hoodlums in. But first, we have to make sure your families are safe. Does that plan make sense to you two?"

Jim said, "Hell, yeah, since we had no plan at all. And I'll go ahead and thank you for both of us for your help."

I smiled and said, "You can thank me if you like, but trust me when I say that Sharon is certainly interested in helping you, but she's also very interested in bringing the guy who tried to attack us to his knees. Winging his arm is not enough for her to be satisfied that she exacted sufficient revenge against the guy."

Sharon also smiled, "Not even close."

Chapter Thirty-Four

Since they had a plan, Jim called Sinclair back and immediately got him on Jim's mother's phone. Sinclair sounded somewhat relieved that Jim had called back rather quickly. He told Jim to bring the treasure up to his mother's home. Sinclair said that he and the rest of his crew would leave the Outer Banks as soon as he had the booty. And he reminded Jim not to involve the police.

Jim didn't trust Sinclair about leaving, but Sharon assured him that there would be little reason for the Jamaicans to attack anyone once they had the loot. She assumed that all the actual mobsters would leave for the island, and it would be next to impossible for U.S. authorities to arrest them down there. She strongly suggested giving the mobsters what they wanted, and there was a good chance they would just leave.

On our way up to the meeting, I got a call from Emily, the FBI agent. She asked how things were going, and I gave her the latest update of the meeting to transfer the treasure. Emily basically agreed that the plan seemed sound, but once I told her about Sinclair, she had additional information.

She said, "I pulled some of what we have on the Jamaican mafia. Lloyd Sinclair is one of the biggest players in the Jamaican mob. He's into the usual: drugs, racketeering, and gambling. He's got a reputation of being a ruthless guy. However, I also have to say that it's pretty unusual for him to make a trip off Jamaica. He usually stays on the island where he feels safe and normally sends his goons if there is any travel off the island. I guess he really covets this treasure booty to come up to the Outer Banks himself."

Suddenly Sharon had an idea. "Emily, any chance you know if this guy has any private planes he uses when he does travel? Doesn't sound like a guy who would take a commercial flight."

Emily looked through her documents and said, "It says here that while he doesn't leave the island that often when he does, he has a corporate jet at his disposal. He allows some of his henchmen to use it for their nefarious needs."

Sharon turned to me and said, "That's how he's going to get off the Outer Banks. We need to find out where the nearest airstrip is in the area. He's not going to a major airport. He is likely to use an unattended one. We need to find out where it is."

That was my queue to do some Googling. I quickly found that there was a small unattended airstrip on the Outer Banks. I said to Sharon, "There's a small unattended strip right in Nags Head."

She said, "I'll bet that's where they're going to leave from. Once we make the drop of the treasure, I'll contact the Nags Head cops, and we'll all converge on the strip. I doubt this guy Sinclair is going to wait very long to leave."

It took us a little over an hour to get to Jim's family's house. We saw a limo and another car that Jim didn't recognize sitting in the driveway. Jim and Henry gathered their treasure booty, and the four of us made our way to the front door.

Jim went to the door to open it, but it was locked. He pushed the doorbell, and Williams opened the door. Williams had an evil grin on his face and said to come in.

Once the four of us were inside, we could see that everyone was huddled in the living room. We immediately recognized Ricketts by the patch on his arm. Sharon said to him, "Damn, I knew I should have gone center mass."

Sinclair said, "I'm Lloyd Sinclair, and that is quite amusing. Perhaps I should give you and Ricketts a few minutes together to stroll down memory lane. I think he would enjoy a bit of a rematch."

Sharon replied, "Anytime he wants another go at me, name the time and place."

Sinclair smirked and said, "Maybe another time, but we are in a bit of a hurry." He turned to Jim and Henry and said, "Do you have the valuables we discussed?"

Jim and Henry both took out their bags of loot and handed them to Sinclair. He opened them and saw that there was quite a bit of jewelry and gold. He smiled and said, "Nice haul here, boys. You seem to have done quite well for yourselves, and now for me."

Sharon said a bit loudly, "So they did their part, now all of you do yours. Get the fuck out of here."

Sinclair said, "Are you in a rush to have us leave?"

"I'm got my hand wrapped around my gun inside my jacket. I can have it out in mere seconds. I think this whole thing needs to end, and the way for that to happen is you leave. Now!"

Sinclair said, "Normally, I would take exception to your tone and probably have you killed, but I see no reason to leave blood all over this beautiful carpet." He turned to everyone in his group and said, "Gentlemen, I think we should take our leave. Oh, one other thing, do not contact the authorities at all. My men are also well-armed, and I doubt the police down in this backwater city know how to handle themselves that well. Simply put, someone will get killed, and I don't think it will be my men. So just go back to your boring little lives and pretend that none of this happened." With that, he and the rest of his crew left the house and headed to the limo and the other vehicle.

As soon as Sinclair was gone, Jim turned to his mom and said, "Mom, are you okay?"

"I'm fine, but who were those guys, and what the hell have you gotten yourself into, Jim?"

Sharon said, "May, I'm sure Jim will give you a full debrief, but not right now." With that, she dialed the Nags Head police department.

The phone rang twice, and a voice said, "Nags Head police department. How can I help you?"

Sharon said, "This sounds like Officer Jones. It's Sharon Levin from Philadelphia."

"It is Jones, but I don't have much to tell you. We haven't made a lot of progress yet."

"No worries. We have through an incredible number of lucky breaks and a little persistence. Ben and I just happened to find Jim and Henry down at Hatteras Island. It was just after a Jamaican mobster named Lloyd Sinclair and his goons had taken Jim's mom hostage. Jim and Henry did have some treasure booty on them, and Sinclair wanted them to bring it up to Nags Head to trade for May's life. Naturally, Jim and Henry didn't hesitate, they asked Ben and me to act as liaisons, and we just handed off the loot to Sinclair and his crew. Everyone here at May's house is safe and secure."

Jones said, "Damn, you have been busy, but why didn't you contact us before now?"

"Sinclair said no cops, and Jim and Henry were worried that your involvement would create some sort of shootout. But we can discuss how I violated the cop's oath by not contacting you, but right now, we need to move. I talked to a colleague with the FBI about Sinclair, and it is likely that he has a private jet on standby and will probably be taking off soon from an unattended airstrip. It looks like Nags Head has the only one nearby. Ben and I are headed over there to find a place to wait. We need you and any other cops who are available to come with us. But we have to go in quiet because we want Sinclair and any of his cronies he's taking with him not to be alerted to our presence."

Jones said, "Damn, you do move fast, Sharon. We know the airstrip, and there is a small hanger where we could be hidden, but how long do you think we can stay there?"

"I'm guessing, but I think the pilot probably stored the jet in Norfolk, so he could refuel. I think Sinclair has already contacted him, and the pilot is readying the jet if he's not already en route. I'm guessing the flight down from Norfolk is less than an hour."

"Brown and I are on our way."

Sharon and I accepted the thanks from Jim, Henry, and May, and we left. I Googled the airstrip location, and when we got there, the place was deserted, but we did see the little hanger. About fifteen minutes later, Jones and Brown showed up.

Sharon said, "Good to see you two. Ready for a little stakeout time?"

Brown said, "Like all good cops, I've got lots of coffee, donuts, and sandwiches at the ready. Let's put our vehicles in the hanger, so one sees us."

We put both vehicles in the hanger, and then it was time to wait. But we didn't have to wait too long. Sharon had been right, and less than thirty minutes later, we heard a small aircraft headed our way. We saw it land and taxi to the end of the runway. Then the pilot just sat.

We saw the limo make its way to the airstrip just thirty minutes later. It parked, and we saw Sinclair and two other Jamaicans exit and made their way to the plane.

Just as they got to the plane, all the armed people, Jones, Brown, and Sharon, came out of the hanger with their guns drawn. Jones yelled, "Put your hands up. You are under arrest. Don't try anything foolish because we will all shoot if you reach for a gun."

Ricketts reached for his weapon, but Sharon fired a round over his head. She said, "I only grazed you last time, but this time I really will go center mass. And it's not dark, so I'm not going to miss."

After just a moment's hesitation, all three raised their hands. Sharon walked over to Sinclair and said, "Nice to see you again." Then she turned to Ricketts and said, "Good decision on your part. Although I sort of wish you had drawn your gun. I would really like to have put a round right through your chest. Oh well, maybe next time."

I smiled and thought that there wouldn't be a next time. These guys were going to prison for a very long time!

Chapter Thirty-Five

After all the Jamaican mobsters were taken into custody, the story of how all of this treasure intrigue transpired came out. First, Bobby, Whyte, and Fitzroy had been left behind by Sinclair with a promise they would get some money when the jewelry was sold. Bobby, Whyte, and Fitzroy had long ago decided that they didn't care if they got any money; they just wanted to get out alive. However, they did have some explaining to do with Jones and Brown.

A short while later, Jim and Henry explained to the police the treasure that Sinclair had taken. They told the police about how they found the treasure and how the two of them, plus Noah, had split some of the treasure. They were told that part of the treasure would be taken as evidence of Sinclair's crime, but Jim and Henry were likely to get that treasure returned. At that point, Jim and Henry came clean about the large cache of jewels and gold they had hidden at Jim's home.

Jim and Henry invited Sharon and me, Officers Brown and Jones, and a Wells Fargo security team to the big unveiling. Naturally, they had their parents also in attendance. We all stood outside the opening, and then Jim started to hand things up to Henry. And he just kept handing things up to Henry. We saw bars of gold. We saw fantastic jewelry, and we even saw some strings of pearls. And they just kept coming. The Wells Fargo security team was in an armored car to protect the baubles, and all the treasure almost filled the armored vehicle.

Once everything had been loaded, the Well Fargo security team took the treasure over to Wells Fargo bank on Croatan Highway. They locked everything in their vault and gave Jim and Henry receipts.

The news of Jim and Henry's treasure find spread quickly. The local news carried a story. Social media went nuts with many women trying to contact Jim and Henry to marry them. However, what became clear quickly was that appraising all this bounty would take a while. In fact, it was at first unclear if the booty belonged to Jim and Henry. However, a North Carolina Archeological Society member went on the news stating that from what he knew, it was very likely that Jim's and Henry's find would ultimately be considered theirs. But it would take a while.

Jim and Henry were besieged with interview requests, but they only took a few. They said that if the treasure were determined to be theirs, they would donate a sizeable sum to Noah's parents and endow several scholarships to Noah's alma mater, East Carolina. In addition, they said they would fund an entire research expedition to see if there was more treasure around the Outer Banks. Finally, they said they would donate a sizeable amount to the local police department for all their help in capturing Sinclair and his cronies and helping keep Jim and Henry safe. In short, they committed to using some of the money, if it ended up being theirs, for various good causes.

While all this hoopla was keeping the Outer Banks and Blackbeard on the front pages of many papers, Sharon and I were just hanging out at the First Colony. We had already extended our stay, so we figured a few more days wouldn't hurt. We had asked Jim, Henry, and the local cops to try to keep our names out of it, and they had done a pretty decent job.

As we were lounging in our hotel room, I said to Sharon, "So Jim called me while you were out walking. He said it is really crazy right now, but he's learned something: Having money is great, but it's nice to try to help people. He said if the booty is eventually determined to be Henry's and his, he's going to send us a big check for all our help."

"I assume you told him that wasn't necessary."

"I did, but he was insistent that they would. So finally, I caved and told him if he did become filthy rich and wanted to do something for us, he could endow a professorial chair at Temple."

"Which you would then accept."

"Uh, no. But I bet I will find I have a bunch of new pals at work if it indeed comes to pass."

"Quite true. So, after all this adventure and danger, what do you want to do for our last couple of days down here?"

"Isn't there a cocktail named sex on the beach? Has vodka, peach schnapps, orange juice, and cranberry juice in it."

Sharon smiled and said, "I do believe there is such a concoction."

"Why don't we get a couple of them to go and then see where that takes us. Maybe the dune-high club will be open!

"Stone, I think that's an excellent way to close out our trip to the Outer Banks!"

About the Author

Steve McMillan has been a management professor for over 25 years but recently turned to writing mysteries. Steve worked in public accounting and real estate before entering academia and uses those experiences coupled with his academic life to develop his stories about accounting and murder. While Steve uses his own life experiences in his character and plot development, he wishes he was as "cool" as Ben Stone. His previous novels in the Accounting series include: *Accounting Can Be Murder, Accounting and Murder Around the World, Accounting for the Blues,* and *Accounting for Vampires.*

The New
Atlantian Library

NewAtlantianLibrary.com or
AbsolutelyAmazingEbooks.com
or AA-eBooks.com